Miniatures

ALSO BY MARIO MILOSEVIC

Animal Life
Claypot Dreamstance
The Coma Monologues
The Doctor and the Clown
Fantasy Life
Kyle's War
The Last Giant
Love Life
Terrastina and Mazolli: A Novel in 99-word Episodes

MINIATURES

Mario Milosevic

For my Mom.
Love,
mario

Ruby Rose's Fairy Tale Emporium • 2012

Miniatures
by Mario Milosevic

Copyright © 2012 by Mario Milosevic

ISBN-13: 978-1470081683
ISBN-10: 1470081687

All Rights Reserved.

The following stories have previously been published, several in slightly different form:

"Red Shift," "The Accountant's Tale," "Excerpts From *A Bestiary of Imaginary Species* by Nenad Dragicevic, Translated by Mario Milosevic," "Don't Even Ask What Freud Would Say," "A Constipation for the Untied States of Amnesia," "The Consequences of Not Averting Your Eyes," "Pulling Strings: A Quantum Story Cycle," and "Sailors Have Long Believed that Magical Things Happen When Ships Cross the Equator,"*conditionalreality. blogspot.com*

"Mother," "Creases," "Fear of Lucille," and "Leaves," *Pulphouse*

"Frames," *Asimov's Science Fiction*

"Be Kind," "Question Authority," "One Morning at the Brew," "Naturalists," and "Housing Project," *Terrastina and Mazolli*

"What They Want," *Poe Little Thing*

"Mark," *Dreams and Nightmares*

"The Chromosome Future" and "The Fatal Colon," *The Magazine of Fantasy and Science Fiction*

"28 Ways to Look at Illness," *annalemma.com*

"This Sentence is the Title of This Story," *Pulphouse Report*

"Moleskin," *qarrtsiluni.com*

"My Administration," *Green Snake Publishing*

"An Unnatural History of Scarecrows," *Bewere the Night*

"The Clex Are Our Friends," *dailysciencefiction.com*

"Genealogy," *Animal Life*

Book design by Mario Milosevic.
Special thanks to Ruth Ford Biersdorf.

No part of this book may be reproduced
without written permission of the author.

Electronic editions of this book are available at most e-book stores.

A production of
Ruby Rose's Fairy Tale Emporium
Published by Green Snake Publishing
www.greensnakepublishing.com

mariowrites.com

CONTENTS

Introduction

9

Red Shift

11

Mother

12

Frames

20

Dragonfly

26

Be Kind

36

The Eulogy Had its Moments,

But Mostly I Had to Get Out of There

37

The Accountant's Tale

45

The Passage of Time

46

What They Want

51

Mark

56

The Iron Tale

58

Question Authority

61

A Somewhat Enigmatic Indication of My Discontent

62

The Chromosome Future

71

The Visitor From the Dark Mountain

72

Creases

78

Excerpts from *A Bestiary of Imaginary Species*

by Nenad Dragicevic

Translated by Mario Milosevic

80

My Origami Summer

88

28 Ways to Look at Illness

97

This Sentence is the Title of this Story

106

Moleskin

110

Don't Even Ask What Freud Would Say

112

One Morning at The Brew

113

My Administration

114

A Constipation for the Untied States of Amnesia

119

Tribal Threads

120

Naturalists

129

The Fatal Colon

130

Deadline

131

The Consequences of Not Averting Your Eyes

142

The Hidden Lives of Puppets

143

An Unnatural History of Scarecrows

151

The Clex Are Our Friends

156

Genealogy

164

Fear of Lucille

169

Housing Project

171

Leaves

172

Solace

176

The Cookie Fortune

180

Pulling Strings: A Quantum Story Cycle

188

Sailors Have Long Believed that Magical Things Happen
When Ships Cross the Equator

194

About the Author

197

INTRODUCTION

I've written a lot of stories since I first thought of writing stories for fun back when I still measured my age in single digits. Some of my favorites have always been the shorter pieces. I like the idea of presenting a world and a story in as few words as possible. How few? A couple of the pieces here are only 50 words long. I maintained a blog for a few years called *Conditional Reality* in which every entry was exactly 100 words long. I've included a few of those here. I've also written an entire novel in 99-word episodes. It's called *Terrastina and Mazolli,* and I've put some of those episodes here as well. Other pieces here are longer than that, but there's nothing more than 2500 words long, which still feels like a miniature to me.

Some of these stories have been published in anthologies, collections, magazines, and websites. Others are original to this volume.

The miniaturist in me already feels like this introduction is getting out of hand, so I'll end it here and send you on to the stories themselves. Enjoy.

RED SHIFT

Splitscreen Ghosthunter turned the universe inside out. Not on purpose; it was just a dream that got away from her. When Splitscreen woke up, the grass, trees, mountains, moon, planets, stars, and galaxies were all nestled within the confines of her skin, humming along like a little machine. Her capillaries, veins, heart, lungs, flesh, and bones were all on the outside, like jellyfish floating in an infinite sea of blood. Far out on the horizon she sensed the remnants of an ancient singularity, her first heartbeats, thrumming insistently. Inside her the voices began. The tiny people started talking to her.

MOTHER

Two days after I buried my mother I went to the garden behind her house and pulled carrots from the ground. I worked slowly, her surviving son, feeling the grit of the earth on my hands, her presence beside me like a ghost. This was her place, the spot on the earth where she felt complete and whole. I needed her loss to hurt me, but I felt no pain. I had anticipated the hurt ever since her doctor found the spot in her brain that blossomed into the tumor that killed her.

Friends said it would hit me when I least expected it. Some small gesture that reminded me of her, a stranger's voice with a hint of her in it, some unexpected detail would trigger a flood of pain and sorrow. I wanted it to happen. I needed to feel that crippling loss and know that something had changed.

My knees were cold from kneeling on the ground and clumps of dirt were wedged under my fingernails. As long as I can remember, my mother had a place in the backyard where she planted seeds, watered the ground, weeded the furrows, and nurtured vegetables to ripeness. I remember my brother Mike used to come out here and get his hands dirty with her. I never caught the gardening bug myself, but it seemed only right that now I should bring in the last harvest.

As I worked I thought about the details I still had to take care of. The lawyers wanted the deed to the house and I didn't know where my mother kept such things. I had to turn off the power to the house. I had to cancel her credit cards, write a stack of thank-you notes. I began to see that society has arranged for the aftermath of a death to be as busy as possible for the survivors. That way they don't have to think about loss and grief.

I picked up the pile of carrots and hugged them to my chest as I stood up and walked into the house.

The phone was ringing and the first thing I thought was that I'll have to have that disconnected too. I considered not answering it because it might have been one of Mom's friends who didn't know, and I would have to be the one to explain it all. But I dropped the carrots into the sink and slapped my hands together to shake off the dirt.

I picked up the phone. "Hello?"

"Neil?"

I felt relieved, then puzzled. Who would be calling me here?

"This is Neil," I said.

"Neil! Is Mom there?"

"Who is this?" I said.

"Who is this? Are you kidding me? It's Mike. Let me talk to Mom."

I hung up the phone and stared at it on the table. Someone's idea of a sick joke. Only it didn't feel like a sicko. It felt real. It felt like Mike. My brother who died twenty-five years ago.

The phone rang again. I let it ring fifteen, twenty times. My head was hot, my palms were slick with sweat. My hands and legs trembled. On the thirtieth ring I picked up the phone.

"Neil, what are you doing?" Still Mike's voice. "Let me talk to Mom."

I didn't say anything. The sound of my own breathing against the telephone receiver seemed to fill the room.

"Neil! Cut it out. Let me talk to Mom."

"Where are you?" I said.

Mike didn't say anything for a while. Then: "I'm not sure. Falling. Stuck in a—a—tumble. It's dark here. Something pulling at me. Where's Mom?"

I closed my eyes and gripped the telephone tighter. *She's three feet away from you,* I wanted to say. *Right where we buried her.*

I coughed, cleared my throat. "She's out," I said. "Getting some stuff for the garden."

"Oh," said Mike. "When's she coming back?"

"I don't know." I swallowed hard. "Soon. How about you?" I said. "When are you coming home?"

"That's just it," said Mike. "I can't. Not without Mom."

"Sure you can," I said. "Come on home, Mike."

"No," said Mike. "I told you. I can't."

"Where are you?"

"Are you okay?" said Mike. "I told you I don't know."

"Don't hang up," I said. I felt sure my desperation came through in my voice.

"Look," said Mike, "just tell her I called. Can you do that?"

"No! I mean, why? Just wait for her. She'll be home soon." *No she won't. Why was I lying to my dead brother?*

14   MARIO MILOSEVIC

"Just tell her, Neil," said Mike. Then he hung up and a dial tone filled my ear.

I hung up the phone and waited for it to ring again. Willed it to ring, but it would not. I sat and stared at it for the rest of the afternoon. Later I pulled up a big chair and curled up into its cushions and thought about my mother.

I remembered when I was twelve. Mike was fourteen. Mom was out in the garden with a kerchief around her head and a trowel in her hand. She sat back on her feet in the black earth and she held up that trowel and pointed it at us.

"I want you boys to have fun," she said, "but I want to know where you are. If you're going to go far, call me. Can you remember to do that?" Then she smiled. We both nodded and hugged her, and she shooed us away and went back to her weeding.

If you're going to go far, call me.

Mike was just doing as he was told. He was calling his mother.

I shivered. He did call, I was sure of it. But what did that mean? Where was he calling from?

I pondered that question as the telephone blurred in my vision and sleep took me like a warm blanket pulling me into a comfortable oblivion.

In the morning the phone call didn't seem as real. Mike's voice didn't replay in my head so convincingly. My neck was sore from sleeping on the chair and my mouth felt gummy. I got out of the chair and went to the backyard. Behind my mother's house there used to be a field, a huge open space where Mike and I and our friends used to play. I stared out over that field now, and watched as a jet plane touched down in the distance. They had built an airport in our field ten years ago. Now the only way to spend time where we used to play was to go to the airport terminal.

I felt hungry.

I got in my car and made the twenty-minute drive to the airport. As I walked from my parking space through the lot to the elevator I thought: *this was our place once.* I felt the years under my feet. I felt Mike and all our friends around me.

I went to one of those restaurants where you get your own tray and cutlery from a rack at one end and collect plates of food from glass cases as you push your tray along a shelf with narrow metal tracks. I followed the line of gatherers and came to the end, where a bored young woman rang up my order. I had only a couple of items on my tray: a sandwich and a glass of water. We used to pick blueberries from bushes around here.

I sat at a table near the entrance. Twenty minutes later my sandwich was eaten and my glass was empty. I fidgeted with the plastic sandwich tray. It crinkled as I bent it in my hands. It made an irritating rattle that I knew annoyed the other diners. I didn't care.

I turned in my seat and watched the planes leaving the earth. They seemed to work so hard to climb into the clouds. I always felt they didn't belong. It was not reasonable to think that something so big, so heavy, could remain in the air. I remembered coming here before the airport was built, before it was even an idea in some developer's head, and how we—my friends and I—would shoot birds with air powered rifles. I never brought down a bird but some of my friends did and they would go over to the fallen creatures and pull off feathers and carry those feathers around for days. I wondered if the bones of any of those birds had been bulldozed under the runway. Maybe they were there now, frozen in the ground, their spirits pushing the big planes up.

I shook my head and realized I had been staring blankly for some time, remembering. I scanned the horizon past the runway. A row of houses, their backyards touching the edge of the airport property, sat like tiny toys in the distance. My mother's house was there.

I used to come here with my friends. Bruce, Noel, Rodney.

And Mike, too.

My brother Mike, who had died soon after turning fourteen. I felt a rush of blood go to my head. Mike had died twenty-five years ago in a bicycle accident. A car turned when it shouldn't have, and Mike tried to brake but skidded instead, slipped under the wheels and died before the paramedics could come.

I remembered his face, saw the baseball cap he always wore: blue and white, the New York Yankees was always his favorite team. I remembered his way of chewing an enormous wad of gum that filled his cheeks the way a clutch of nuts fills a chipmunk's mouth. He was a good shot with the BB gun, too. He got a few birds. Always felt great after shooting a bird. Loved to kill them. Loved to see them fall from the sky. He hooted and whooped as he bounded over bushes and grass to where the bird had fallen. I never followed. Couldn't stomach it. Couldn't see the *point.*

I went back to the counter. Got a glass of water. I didn't remember what I thought the day he died. Hadn't thought about the day he died for a long time. Not until last night. After the phone call.

Bruce was there, the day Mike died. He saw it. Saw the whole thing. He said Mike only said one word as gravity pulled his bike out from under him and slammed him to the pavement.

"Mama."

That was it. That was the whole thing, that was the last thing he said, probably the last thing he thought.

I thought about that word. "Mama." When they find black boxes from crashed planes and they play the tapes of people who know they are about to die, people who aren't kids anymore, who have lived a life away from their parents' house for years, pilots and cockpit crew, they say, "Mother." When soldiers are dying on battlefields, people who have been there and have seen it, heard it, they say that dying men scream for their mothers even as their bodies are torn apart and their blood spills into the mother of us all: the earth.

I wrapped my hands around the glass on the table. It was cool and slippery. I left it there and got up and walked out of the restaurant. I went to the parking tower and got in my car. A jet split the air above my head.

My mother died five days ago. Mike died twenty-five years ago. Was all that was left of them now what I carried inside me? Was that why the phone call came last night? Was Mike trying to come back? Or just saying good-bye?

I got into my car and drove away from the airport. On the way home I stopped the car along the freeway and parked on the shoulder. I stepped out and walked a few hundred feet into the woods. I kneeled down and put my hands into the rich cool wet earth and held my mother for a few minutes. My tears dropped on the leaves. Cold moisture circled my knees. I felt Mike around me, felt his pain, felt my grief like a blanket begin to press against me and fill my heart like warm cotton. It was heavy and close and needed.

I fell forward and my cheek touched the ground. "Mama," I whispered.

FRAMES

#1

Janet found an unexposed roll of super 8 film in the box of odds and ends her father had sent to her with a note that read: Here is some stuff I don't need anymore. Maybe you can find a use for it. The film was still in its airtight yellow pouch. Janet pushed aside an old quilt her grandmother had made years ago and found the dusty old super 8 camera her father had used for mental Olympics competitions, piano recitals, birthday parties, and vacations. This was before camcorders and VCRs. Janet set up the camera on a tripod in the living room, training the lens on the maple tree in the front yard.

#2

The camera had a stop-motion button that exposed one frame at a time. Janet loaded the film, attached the remote release cable to the stop motion button, and clicked a picture of the tree. It was late afternoon. Sweet light, she remembered a photographer on a television talk show once called it. The sun low, the air clear, the light golden, almost solid. The leaves on the maple tree illuminated like actors on a stage. She nodded. Sweet light.

#3

Janet stirred vegetables around a wok and remembered being told when she was two years old that she was a genius, a prodigy. She was able to speak several languages by the time she was three, invented calculus by age four, and composed and performed symphonies at five. Her parents had high hopes for her, but she was more interested in her friends.

#4

She created her friends the day after her third birthday party, when her father had told her she needed to stop having fun and spend more time with her math books. She thought and thought and thought about what kind of friends she wanted to have. She wanted them to like her. She wanted them to be smaller than her. She wanted them to pay attention to her. There were about a dozen of them, and they did all those things. After that, Janet's friends would come around occasionally and take her away from her genius activities. Her father fretted whenever she spent this time with her friends. Janet, he said, you need to keep up with your studies. You could be the greatest mind the world has ever seen.

#5

Janet turned off the stove and went to the camera and snapped another frame. Then she went back to the kitchen and poured the vegetables over a plate of rice. She ate slowly, in dim light, glancing up at the wall clock every few minutes. By the time she finished her meal, she was in complete darkness. The moon cleared the horizon a few minutes later. Its silvery light seemed cold, but interesting. She rose and snapped off two more frames.

#6

At the supermarket where she worked the midnight to seven a.m. shift, Janet smiled at the customers and pulled their groceries over the laser scanner. Someone looked at her with that glint of recognition she had grown to hate. Say, he said, aren't you that girl, that genius? Janet felt her face turn red, and silently cursed the local reporter who had unearthed her story and published a recent snapshot along with pictures of her at the mental Olympics television show from thirty years ago. Everyone tells me that, said Janet, but would a genius be working at a Safeway? I mean, really! The man laughed and picked up his change and groceries. I guess you're right, he said, but you sure do look like her. Janet remembered the super 8 camera on the tripod at home.

#7

Janet bought a pint of ice cream and a spiral bound notebook after she punched out. She got home as the sun was rising. She sat on the couch in her living room and studied the maple tree as she ate the ice cream. The tree looked as cold as her hands felt holding the carton. She stood and walked to the camera and held the remote cable in her hand. She exposed five frames, spaced a minute apart, then recorded the date and time of each exposure in her notebook. Later, she brought the notebook up to date by recording the dates and times of the first three exposures.

#8

Janet's father phoned her and asked if she'd found any use for the box of odds and ends. I don't know, Dad, she said, I used the movie camera. Do you think that was a good idea? Her father hesitated, then said, Sure Janet, sure. You're really going to be something. Do you know that? You're going to be someone great, someone people will talk about for a long long time. Janet's friends came into the living room then. She dropped the phone and told them all about the movie she was making. It's going to take me a whole year! she said. They nodded and clapped their little hands and she hugged them tight.

#9

Janet played with her friends for the rest of the morning. She felt flush with joy as they each pressed the button on the camera several times, and she carefully recorded each frame in her notebook. The tree will change over time, she said. The leaves will turn color and fall off, the branches will get snow on them, the buds will come back after winter and then the leaves will grow again. It'll be a cycle. Then we can play the movie and watch the tree change over time. Won't that be fun? Her friends nodded.

#10

Janet's friends left soon after noon. Janet was too tired to try to talk them into staying. Come back, she said. We will, said her friends. As long as you remember us.

MINIATURES

#11

Janet's boss said she was doing an excellent job. You're so good, Janet, he said. I'll never understand for the life of me why you, a genius, wants to work here, but I'm glad you do. You're so good. Janet nodded and tried to smile, but it was not the same as smiling at the customers. She wanted this job too much, she had to be too nice. It wasn't fair that people thought she was so smart. It wasn't fair. It was like they wanted her to think she was a failure. She thought about her notebook. It was almost all she thought about as she spent her nights scanning people's groceries. She had begun to embellish her notebook with comments about her feelings and her state of mind at the moment each frame was snapped.

#12

A year after she started, the movie was finished. According to Janet's notebook, the film was exactly one thousand, six hundred, and forty five frames long. Less than two minutes. She got the film developed, then set up the projector so that the movie would show on her living room wall.

#13

Janet made popcorn dripping with butter, sprinkled with salt. She waited for her friends to come. When they arrived, they snuggled around her like kittens. They were soft and warm and cuddly. Janet thought of all the people over the years who said she was a genius. She wasn't. She just knew how to make friends. She reached over and snapped on the projector. The wall counted down numbers: five four three two. Then a beep and a crackle.

#14

The maple tree was like a sculpture on the wall, jerkily growing from a lushly green thicket of leaves to a smear of orange, yellow, red, then a frosty white, a stark crooked outline against the sky, and finally a fresh green thicket again. Then the wall became bright white and the film spooled through the projector to the end. Janet did not snap off the projector. She felt tears well up in her eyes. She wanted to tell her friends that *that* was the genius. The *tree* was genius. She wasn't. She just knew how to make friends. It was a good movie, said the friends. We really liked it. She hugged them and they stayed for a long time. Janet was as happy as she ever remembered being in her life.

#15

When they disappeared again, Janet saved the film in a little canister and put it away for safekeeping. She spent many hours reading over her notebook. It *was* a good film; it had brought her friends back. That knowledge filled her with joy.

#16

Eventually, she started thinking about a new project to bring her friends back. She was pretty sure they would like a replica of the Golden Gate Bridge made out of toothpicks. After her next shift at the supermarket, she bought several dozen boxes of toothpicks and a lot of glue.

DRAGONFLY

"I am a symbol of illusion," said the dragonfly to Ivan. "So you figure out if you are really talking to me or if this is all just . . . an illusion."

The sun was high and felt hot on Ivan's head. His wife Jill and son Tim were down by the lake, a short distance away. They had left him here, at the picnic table, after their lunch, to finish the last cigarette of his life. He was quitting for the sake of his five-year-old son. To set an *example*.

Now this. A talking dragonfly, perched on the edge of the table, looking up at him, with its wings barely pulsing back and forth. Ivan leaned forward and studied the lace-like pattern on the insect's wings and sipped his glass of orange soda, wishing it was something stronger. If he had been drunk then all this would have made sense. But a talking dragonfly when he was sober? That took some thinking about. He inhaled two lungfuls of smoke from his cigarette, which looked to be about half finished. An inch or two more and an old life would be left behind. A new life begun.

The dragonfly sported a lovely blue body, shimmery, like some exotic cloak. It had landed near the edge of a paper plate smeared with the remains of Tim's franks and baked beans.

"Done yet?" asked the dragonfly.

"Done what?"

"Thinking about all this. Are you finished? Can I get on with my pitch?"

"Not so fast," said Ivan. "First, how come you can talk?"

"Reincarnation. I used to be a human being. When I died I ended up here in this dragonfly."

"No," said Ivan. "I mean, how can you talk? Dragonflies don't have vocal chords."

"Smart aleck, huh? Okay, it's a telepathy thing. I think my sentences and you hear them in your head like they were words spoken aloud."

Ivan nodded. "Of course."

"Happy now?"

Ivan waved his hand. "Fire away." He took a short puff on his cigarette, then blew the smoke at the dragonfly.

"Do you mind?" said the dragonfly. "I hate that. When I was a person I'd have smacked you silly for blowing smoke at me."

"Oh," said Ivan. "An anti-smoking nut, eh? That's rich, coming from a bug named for a fire-breathing creature." He blew more smoke at the dragonfly. He would never have this pleasure again. It felt good to blow smoke in someone's face.

"Now I remember why I hated you butt fiends," said the dragonfly.

Ivan grinned. "Talk to me, illusion."

"Here's the thing," said the dragonfly, sounding annoyed, "I don't like this particular link in the chain of life. I want out, and I mean now. I need you to kill me so I can go on to the next life."

"Kill you?"

MINIATURES

27

"The sooner the better."

"That's crazy. Why would you want to die? If I were you I wouldn't want to die. You can fly, for Chrissake. Everyone *dreams* of flying."

"Not me. Vertigo. I hated it when I was human; now it's worse. I get real dizzy when I fly and flying's about the only way dragonflies get around. You see what I'm up against?"

Ivan considered this. "Okay. But what do you need me for? Can't you just fly into something dangerous like a hot light bulb or a camp fire or something? There must be zillions of ways to fry yourself."

Ivan thought he almost felt the dragonfly shudder.

"No," said the dragonfly. "I want it done quick. One good stomp with a boot, your boot, and everything will be fine again. Besides, suicide is a sticky situation. No one who's ever killed themselves comes back much higher than a flea for a long long time. Mosquito, tops."

Ivan puffed thoughtfully on his cigarette, this time being careful to blow the smoke away from the dragonfly. "If I do this little thing for you won't I get bad karma and come back as some lesser species when *I* kick off?"

"Come on," said the dragonfly. "You haven't killed any bugs in your life before today? One more or less won't make a bit of difference. Besides which, I'm betting you don't even believe in reincarnation."

"Got me there," said Ivan.

"Thought so," said the dragonfly.

"I'm not even sure I believe in *you*."

"Fair enough," said the dragonfly. "So killing me wouldn't

mean a thing, right? Either way, I win. So let's get it done."

"Life and death," said Ivan. "It's a funny business isn't it?"

"Ha ha. A laugh riot. Are you with me on this, or aren't you?"

"My wife says I've got to stop smoking or I'll die. So I have a choice. What choice would you make?"

"I'm making a choice right now. You going to help me?"

"Thing is, I like smoking. But I know she's right. Bad example for my son. If I keep smoking, I'm telling him that life isn't worth preserving. It isn't worth cherishing."

"Fascinating," said the dragonfly. "You have some absorbing issues in your life that demand your attention. So let's get this little favor for me out of the way so you can get back to them."

"Look at you," said Ivan. "You're choosing death. Begging for it in fact, without even knowing what's coming next. You'd rather play reincarnation roulette and take your chances on a next life than make the best of this one."

"I believe I've explained that."

Ivan was about to take another puff of the cigarette then stopped himself. He focused his attention on the dragonfly. "Can I save your wings?"

"My wings?"

"As a kind of trophy. I like the pattern."

"Oh great. I find the one guy in the world who's the great white bug hunter. You want my wings, pal, you got 'em."

"But I don't want to step on them," said Ivan. "I mean that would damage them."

MINIATURES

29

"Maybe I better find someone else for this," said the dragonfly.

"No no," said Ivan. "Really. I like you. I want to do this for you. I promise I'll make it quick."

The dragonfly sighed. "Okay," it said glumly.

Ivan put his cigarette down on the picnic table so the tip hung over the edge. A thin stream of smoke curled from it into the air. Less than an inch left of the cigarette now. What was that—one good long puff? Maybe two or three if he was careful and rationed them out. It made Ivan, at that moment, think of a genie coming out of a lamp. Crazy thought. He wiped his fingers on his shirt to get rid of the grease residue, then leaned over and grasped one of the dragonfly's wings. He could barely feel it between his thumb and forefinger.

"Did you get it?" asked the dragonfly. "Is my wing gone?"

Ivan held his breath. "Just getting situated," he said. He pulled as gently as he could. The wing separated from the dragonfly without fuss or sound. Indeed, with no perceptible resistance at all. "There," said Ivan. "I got it. Did that hurt?"

"Not a bit." The dragonfly sounded amazed. "I can't see behind there, did you get it all intact?"

"Well sure I did," said Ivan. "What do you think, I'm an amateur?" He put the wing down on a paper napkin. It almost disappeared in the white fibers. "Now the rest of them," he said. He worked quickly, plucking the remaining wings in turn and placing them next to the first one on the napkin. The dragonfly seemed to relax.

"It's really happening, isn't it?" said the dragonfly.

"All done," said Ivan when he had placed the last one. "I've got your wings right here." He picked up the dragonfly and placed it on the ground.

"I can hardly believe it!" said the dragonfly. "I'm finally going to die."

"This is really your wish?" said Ivan.

"Yes," said the dragonfly. "Oh yes. I wish I could close my eyes."

"I hope you get what you want," said Ivan. He raised his foot, then paused. He let it back down on the ground.

"Vertigo," he said. "That's a bummer. I feel bad for you, I really do." Ivan raised his foot again and held it just over the dragonfly. "Here I go," he said. "Last chance to back out."

"New life, here I come!" said the dragonfly.

Ivan put his foot down slowly beside the dragonfly.

"It's probably some trauma you've been carrying around from life to life," he said. "The vertigo, I mean. You'll probably have it in your next life, you know. Sure. Stands to reason. You had it as a human and you still have it as a dragonfly. You probably need to work it out or something."

"What's with the talk show psychology? Do it!"

Ivan looked down at the dragonfly. His foot hovered in the air. The muscles in his legs began to tremble slightly. The motion reminded him of insect wings, trembling in air, vibrating with the wind.

"No," he said. "I can't do it. It wouldn't be fair. You've got to do what you've got to do. You have to figure this out on your own. I can't help you by killing you."

He leaned back on the picnic table bench and picked up

MINIATURES

31

his cigarette, intending to inhale its smoke into his lungs. He held the thing up, brought it close to his lips, then changed his mind and ground it out on the paper plate. Then he drained the last couple of swallows from his soda can and tossed it across the grass to a garbage can.

"You bastard!" screamed the dragonfly. "You rip off my wings then leave me here on the ground where I'm just going to starve to death! You bloody piece of—"

"Oh shut up," said Ivan. "You've got a life. Deal with it."

"I wanted to *get* a life. You said you would help me."

"You don't have to die to get a life. Look at me, I'm a new man. Started a completely new way of living. If that isn't a new life, what is? You could do the same thing, you know."

"I don't have any *wings*."

"Yeah," said Ivan. "Sorry about that."

"Who are you talking to, Dad?"

Ivan turned around to see Tim and Jill walking up hand in hand. Their hair was slicked down on their heads. Fresh from a lake swim, they seemed to float on the grass, hovering like giant bugs.

"Just a friend of mine," said Ivan. Tim climbed up on the picnic table. Jill sat beside him. She looked at the bent cigarette on the paper plate.

"Was it really your last one?" she said.

"Promise," said Ivan. "No more smoking."

Tim noticed the wings on the napkin. He picked up the napkin and held the wings close to his eye.

"Careful with that," said Ivan.

Tim lifted the napkin in the air, grasped one corner of it, and shook it so the wind blew it open. Ivan could not see the dragonfly wings, but they must have been caught by the wind and blown away.

Tim saw them. He pointed at the air and squealed. "There go the wings," he said.

Ivan felt a pang of regret. He really wanted to keep those wings. He could have preserved them in a block of plastic or something and kept them as a reminder of the time his life changed.

He stared at the air, straining to see the wings, but it was no use. They were gone.

When he let his eyes return to the picnic table, Tim was gone. The spot where Jill had been sitting was empty.

A voice, small but distinct, called up to him from the ground. "That's what you need?" it said. "Some made up family to keep you honest?"

"They're not made up," said Ivan to the dragonfly.

"They're not real. At least not now. If they ever were."

Ivan looked down at the ground. "Where are you?"

"Right where you left me just as your courage decided to take wing and leave you high and dry. Not to mention me."

Ivan laughed. "You look ridiculous. Without your wings."

"How about I rip off your arms and laugh at you, dick wad. How'd you like that?"

Ivan pulled a pack of cigarettes from his pocket. The logo was a blue dragonfly. He shook a smoke onto his palm, placed it between his lips and lit it.

MINIATURES

"I have a proposition for you," he said.

"I can't wait to hear it," said the dragonfly.

"You help me quit, and I'll help you die." He pulled in a billowing breath of smoke, let it fill his lungs, then blew it straight at the dragonfly.

"How am I supposed to do that?" said the dragonfly. "You obviously love smoking more than you love life."

Ivan remembered the day his girl friend, Jill, had told him there was no future for them. They couldn't get married, could not have children, could not have a *life* together unless he quit smoking. That was five years ago. He still thought about Jill. And the son they might have had. A lot.

The bug had a point. Ivan really did like his cigarettes. Reveled in them. Loved the feel of smoke raking through his windpipe and nostrils. The satisfying buzz that nicotine gave him. All of it seemed like the perfect excuse for living a life.

What did this dragonfly know? It couldn't even fly anymore.

"Sorry about your wings," said Ivan.

"Just finish what you started," said the dragonfly. "It can't be that hard, can it?"

Ivan had a vague awareness of his life continuing on from this moment. It was as though he had determined to watch himself, watching this dragonfly. He drew in more smoke, held it in his lungs for as long as possible. Longer. It felt like a piece of dough lodged in his chest. He never wanted to let it go. *Never*.

Not even to blow it into the dragonfly's eyes.

Which were turned up towards him, as though the insect

wanted something from Ivan. As though it could get whatever it needed, whatever that might be, from someone too stupid to quit smoking.

He rose from his sitting position at the picnic table, and towered over the de-winged creature. What must it be like, to fly, and then not fly? What was it to have the capacity, then to lose it forever?

He lifted his foot, and with it, his heavy boot. Then placed it squarely on top of the dragonfly and ground the sole into the grass, pressing with all his might as he exhaled smoke into the air.

Ivan coughed twice, spit out black sputum, and turned red from the exertion.

"Here's to life," he said.

BE KIND

Terrastina goes to the library to use one of their free internet computers. She wants to know about the world wide web. It's the only frontier we have now, says the woman at the computer next to her. Really? asks Terrastina. Oh yeah, says the woman. I've found a web site where people can send messages to the stars. You type in what you want to say to aliens. The site stores the messages and then every week or so they beam them into space. Terrastina logs onto the site and waits for some inspiration to come to her.

THE EULOGY HAD ITS MOMENTS, BUT MOSTLY I HAD TO GET OUT OF THERE

Why am I telling you any of this? Tell me about yourself. Have you always loved stories? Most kids do. They'll listen to the same one over and over. Must be comforting to them. I was too young to have children of my own. But I'll try to tell you a story. I know a pretty good one. Listen and you'll probably recognize it.

My mother always told me that funerals were for the living. When I got really sick, just before the end, I thought about that a lot. I was proud that I didn't convert to any religion. Life long atheist, I wasn't about to throw away my principles just because I ended up in a fox hole that many had been to before.

When you are young and healthy, it's almost fun to think about your funeral. Who would be there, where it would take place, the eulogy, the crying. When you've been given a death sentence, it's all different. Suddenly all those things are heavy with meaning. Cremation or burial? It didn't matter to me, but my parents might have issues with either choice. Service or no service? Again, immaterial to my rotting corpse, but people need to know, they need to see, get it fixed in their minds. Church or funeral home? My mother believes in God. She'd

MINIATURES

want it in a church. Who was I to deny her that smallest of comforts in the midst of my passing? I was so young, only sixteen. A real tragedy for my parents, what with my unfulfilled potential and everything. So I agreed to a traditional funeral, in a church, and no cremation afterward. I even went for the headstone, with my name chiseled into it. And my dates. She brought me the catalog. I picked out a nice gray marble one.

Okay, I see you cringing. Understandable. But my parents are old world. They did not grow up in an antiseptic culture that denied, postponed, ignored, and softened death. My father has an album of photographs of *his* father's home funeral. Snapshot after snapshot of my grandfather lying in a homemade coffin in his living room, scores of neighbors and families clustered around, some of them mugging for the camera.

And even though I am making this all up for you, to ease your life a little, well, it is also mostly true, in its way.

What? You're confused? Why? We really *did* have a different view of death. We really *did* pick out our own headstones. But I have to tell this story carefully. Because of who you are.

Tell me some more. How old are you?

Only five? Funny. When I pushed you out of the way of that car, I thought you were older. Seven, maybe. No matter. I've never been good with ages. Think every child is seven and every adult is 38. When you get older you'll understand.

Yeah, I have my own way of looking at the world. It's probably different from other people's. But that's because of my circumstances. They're kind of unique.

Oh, sure, everyone's unique in the world. We all are. But

I'm *really* different now. I see things in a completely different way.

So, what about school?

Kindergarten, huh? Morning or afternoon?

Yeah, I remember I was in the morning. That was better. I liked it better than the afternoon. Well, I think I did. I don't really remember, it was so long ago. I think because I'm a morning person now I figure I must have liked that then, too, but who knows? Maybe I didn't even know there was an afternoon kindergarten.

Okay, yeah, I'm getting kind of boring for you. I know. But you're the only one who has seen me, so far.

I look kind of funny, don't I? The injuries from the car hitting me. I'll try to keep that part away from you. Must be kind of scary. You remember the car, don't you?

Oh. You mean I look funny because you can see through me? Okay, I guess that is kind of funny. Scary, too?

Well, sure, maybe a little. It's not everyday you see a ghost, is it?

Your mom was at my funeral. I guess you know that. My mom wanted to say something to her, but I don't think she did. Mothers have this connection, I've observed. They share emotions only they can know about.

You want to be a mother? Well, sure. I know most little girls want to grow up and have babies.

Twelve? Wow. That's a lot of babies.

Sure, if you want, you can put your hand through me. I think it would be okay.

No, I didn't feel a thing.

You didn't either? But you're not scared, right? There's no reason to be scared. I don't really know why I'm here. At the funeral, it was getting to be, well, pretty boring, if you want to know the truth. I was never much for rituals and stuff, and funerals are just one long ritual. For the living. I said that before, didn't I?

You are right, I shouldn't be talking about death to a little girl. But I shouldn't be here, either. Don't get me wrong. I'm glad I saved your life and everything, that's not what I mean. Say, come to think of it, why did you run into the street like that?

Chasing a ball. Ha ha. Of course. Classic.

Why did I run after you? Well, I saw that car coming at you. The driver didn't see you. I knew you would be hurt. Really bad. I knew I was going to be hurt, too, but you know I already had a death sentence on me. I had this terminal disease, so my loss wasn't going to be much. A few months, maybe. It's easy to be brave when you don't have much to lose. No one at the funeral said anything about that. Too honest, I guess. Funerals are not always the best place to look for honesty.

I know you think you would have been safe. We all think we'll be safe forever. I did. I figured I'd grab you up and just run out of the way.

No, it didn't happen quite the way I expected. I wrapped you up and tried to run, but I stumbled.

You don't remember that? Just me holding you? I remember you starting to cry just as the bumper caught my side. I held you. I knew I was in trouble but I held you, wrapped you in my arms to protect you.

Listen, the papers called me a hero.

How do I know? I overheard some people at my funeral, that's how.

Leaving the funeral? That was easy. I was getting *so* bored that I just kind of sat up. Just to shake off the sleepiness, you know? There was a little tug, like maybe how you have to pull on licorice with your teeth before a piece will come off, and then I was free. Once I sat up everything seemed better. So I tugged my legs out one at a time, and hopped down from the coffin. The minister was still droning on about how I risked my life for a stranger. How heroic it was. Blah blah blah. That was ancient history to me by then.

Because suddenly I was in a new world. I was as free as just about anyone can be. I started walking away. And then I ended up here.

I don't know how long it took. Time kind of changed. I don't know what day it is or what year it is. It's kind of nice, actually. Easy.

Oh. Your favorite doll is this one? Yeah, that's a nice one. Thank you for showing me. I like the red hair. Very cute.

The past? Sure I think about it. A little. Doesn't everyone?

My toys were more in the area of spaceships and baseballs. Things curving over the Earth I guess you might say.

Yeah, kind of like what I'm doing now.

I've heard of theories like that. Everything is happening at once. The past is still here. The future is already here. We all exist cheek by jowl with every era that ever was or ever will be. Einstein or someone like that, right?

MINIATURES

Say, you're pretty smart for a little girl. How'd you know about all these theories and things?

I did kind of notice that there were some odd things in your house. Like that doodad over there. What is that? I looks like a kind of souped-up microwave or something.

A teleporter, eh? I used to pretend things were other things, too.

No. Not a real one.

You aren't kidding?

So, um, what do you teleport?

Medicine. Okay. You need medicine. Oh, man, you're sick? Is it bad?

That's a relief. I want you to live a long time. I want you to live forever, basically. That's what I wanted when I ran out to save your life.

I kind of noticed that, too. It looks like one of those exercise machines that people buy to make them do exercise. My father always said he wanted one. So my Mom bought him one and he used it about two times and then it just sat in our garage. My mother said it was a dust magnet and that was about the end of that. She was going to have a garage sale to get rid of it.

Did she ever? I don't know. Not before I died, anyway.

What's that? I must have misheard you. It's *not* an exercise machine? Then what is it?

A robot assistant. You're pulling my leg. Why would a little girl need a robot assistant? Oh! You were injured in the accident. Is that it? You didn't want to tell me, though. I'm so sorry. I wanted so much for you to be okay.

Oh, sorry. I don't listen sometimes. I was going to work on that, you know. My mother said men are like that a lot. They don't listen. She had books on the subject. How men and women are so different.

Yeah. She said that too. Men don't see things. But I'm not a man, I used to tell her. I'm just a boy. She got a kick out of that, how I was so clever, she said. How I was going to be so smart. That's what she always said.

Your mother died? Hey, I'm sorry about that. But wait a minute. I just saw your mother. At the funeral.

No, no. That was just a few minutes ago. I told you I left the funeral and then I came here. Not on purpose, or anything, my feet just kind of took me here.

Okay, I'll just shut up and listen for a minute. You have a story for me, right?

—

Wow. Is all that true? *You* pulled me out of the funeral? You wanted to see me? And it's now—what did you say?— ninety years after. It took ninety years for me to make that trip. So then you're not a little girl anymore, are you? You're an old lady. Not *five* but *ninety*-five. Geez. My perception must be off. That's how it is when you're a ghost: everything is different. You see old people as young people. Oh, sorry. My mother told me not to call people old. Sorry, sorry.

But you *look* like you're just a little girl.

Oh I get it. I see what I remembered of you. Rose-colored glasses and all that, right? I see what I want to see.

Oh. Okay. Hey, you're welcome. I didn't want to die or anything that day, but I'm glad you lived such a long life.

MINIATURES

No, I don't mind if you cry. But really, you don't have to cry for me.

Afraid? You don't really have to be afraid. Once you die it's all different, but the same, too. You know what I mean? Things kind of lock into place. It's comfortable.

No, no. I'm glad you had me over.

I'd like to offer you some tissue, but in my present state, that's kind of impossible.

When are they coming over? Oh, they come everyday? That's nice they visit.

You didn't want to go live with them? I can see that. Independence, right? You want to live your own life.

Oh, hey, I understand if you're tired. I get tired, too. Or I got tired. I don't know. It's confusing. Comfortable, like I said, but confusing.

No, really, it was no bother at all. I hope you got what you wanted.

Yeah, it's been nice talking to you again. Or, actually, for the first time.

You don't want it to end. I understand. I don't either. I don't want anything to end. Not anymore. All we have are stories, after a while. When they end, there's nothing left.

Bye. I love you, too.

Sweet dreams.

I love you, too.

THE ACCOUNTANT'S TALE

We were working on a complicated account involving the judicious concealment of offshore assets when we realized one from our team had been absent for days. Her cubicle was eerily empty, only a snapshot of her dog to indicate a living being had ever been there. We called her house, but there was no answer. We sent her an email, inquiring as to her whereabouts. We heard nothing for weeks. Then, after work on the account was completed, a moving company arrived and took the picture of her dog. We were all relieved that the photo was finally accounted for.

THE PASSAGE OF TIME

My neighbor has some peculiar ideas about food. He likes to barbecue clocks and watches, which is completely wrong. Timepieces should be roasted in an oven. That way the seconds get all crunchy and the minutes remain juicy while the hours get this heady aroma that fills the house. Makes my mouth water just thinking about it.

But fine. The man invites me for barbecue so I go over for some barbecue.

I bring an old watch I don't use anymore. Its face is all scratched up, plus it requires batteries to operate. I don't usually tolerate such devices. Watches should be wound. If you don't have a hand in making your own time piece tick, then the gears and springs are nothing but hunks of metal when they should be reflections of you and your personality. I feel very strongly about this.

I find the neighbor at his house standing over a barbecue grill. He's tending to a big red alarm clock that is beginning to melt a little in a way that I have to admit makes me want to have a taste.

The neighbor claps me on the back when he sees me and grabs my hand and shakes it as though I'm his long lost son or something. People can be that way sometimes. They want you to be their friend so bad that they go a little overboard.

He takes the watch from me and examines it carefully. "Wow," he says, "this is a nice watch. You sure you want to barbecue it?"

I am not sure at all. I don't exactly want to keep it, but I don't particularly approve of barbecuing it either. I do not, however, see the need to tell my neighbor my complete thoughts on the matter.

"Absolutely," I say. "I can't wait."

He throws it on the grill next to the alarm clock. It begins to sizzle immediately. Juices ooze out of it and splatters on the coals under the grill. Flames shoot up and coat the watch. It begins browning nicely. The smell of it invades my nostrils. I begin to see the wisdom of barbecuing.

My neighbor takes deep breaths. "Oh, that smells good," he says. Then he slaps a can of beer in my hand. "When you're finished with that one," he says, "I got lots more." He grins.

I smile back at him, crack open the can, and take a sip.

I look around the yard. There are no other guests. This makes me a little nervous. My neighbor sees my discomfort.

"Nope," he says. "No one else accepted my invitation. It's just you and me."

"Ahh," I say in as neutral a tone as I can manage.

"Can you believe people are still nervous about cooking their clocks and watches and things?"

"It's a mystery," I say.

"The way I see it, with time slipping away like they say it is, why not enjoy it while it's still here? It'll be gone soon enough, right?"

"Right."

MINIATURES

My neighbor walks over to a table set a few feet from his barbecue grill. He's got more clocks on the table. Some of them hang over the edge, drooping and oozing toward the lawn. Which means they are not fresh. No clock in optimal condition would do that. My neighbor picks up one of them and throws it on the grill next to the alarm clock and my watch, which I now see is embarrassingly small. I should have brought something bigger.

"How you like your clock?" he says. "Rare, I'll bet."

"Well done," I say.

"Huh," he says. "I would have figured you for rare. Would have bet my life on it."

"Nope," I say. "Used to like it rare, but that was when I was younger and more foolish."

He grabs the clock with his tongs and turns it over. It has lines on the other side, from the grill. The clock also displays a decidedly greenish tinge. Completely unappetizing. I begin concocting plausible excuses that will get me out of my neighbor's yard with grace and haste.

"My cousin likes it well done," he says.

"Oh," I say. "Is that so?"

"Yeah. Of course, I never liked my cousin much."

"That's too bad," I say.

"Yeah. Too bad."

My neighbor's yard is littered with clock gears. They attract birds. The birds snatch up the gears and fly away with them.

My neighbor becomes thoroughly involved with fussing over the grill. The coals get redder and redder.

"You know what," I say.

My neighbor grunts.

"I just remembered. I have to call my mother. It's her birthday, and I completely forgot."

"Oh yeah," he says. "You don't want to forget your mother's birthday."

"Exactly," I say. "I'll just go back to the house and give her a call."

My neighbor looks relieved that I won't be staying.

"By the time you get back," he says, "your watch will be done. As a side dish. The clock will be well done too. Exactly the way you like it." He looks up from the grill and stares me right in the eye. "That *is* the way you like it, right?"

What can I tell him? That I wish he lived somewhere else? That he makes me so nervous and skittish I want to scream whenever I see him? Or that when he arrived in the neighborhood things got to be so different that I didn't know who I was anymore? Could I tell him any of these things?

"Absolutely," I say. "Don't worry, I'll be back. I know what it is to cook a meal for people. It would be rude of me not return. I won't do that to you. I won't be a rude neighbor."

My neighbor slams the cover of his grill shut.

"Forget it," he says. "I only asked you over to be polite. Screw polite. I don't want to be polite."

The beer can, still cold in my hand, suddenly feels like a burden too heavy to carry. I lay it down on the table next to his grill. My neighbor is completely still. He's like a freeze frame at the end of a movie. I maneuver past him and lift up the grill top. I use his tongs to retrieve my watch. It is charred and beat-up looking, but it is mine and I want it back.

I leave my neighbor's yard with my watch.

Inside my house I look through the window at my neighbor. He is still frozen in place.

I put my watch down on the cutting board in my kitchen to let it cool.

It is hard to say how long I leave it there. My mother phones me. We talk, catch up on what's going on. I hang up and go into the kitchen. The watch is melted into the cutting board.

I put my hands to my face.

My left wrist holds a white band that goes all around. It is the place where my watch used to be.

I think about what it will take to remove the watch from my cutting board.

My neighbor, I see through my window, falls over onto his lawn. He is frozen stiff. His hands stick up into the air like sundial gnomons.

WHAT THEY WANT

"You know what got us here, don't you, Alex?" asked Mandi. She floated next to the window looking out across space to the distant moon, just beginning to wax into a crescent.

Alex floated beside her. "Luck," he said.

The curve of the earth, glowing dark blue and iridescent in twilight, crawled slowly under them, matching the motion of the space station.

"Nope," said Mandi. She touched her temple. "It was the coil in here. The most complex structure in the universe."

Alex shrugged. "If you say so," he said, "but *I* remember that lottery thing. You were there, as I recall. We bought a ticket, remember?"

"That's just a trifling detail," said Mandi. "It's the way the manifest world got us here, but the *real* real world—the one that is hidden and makes things right—it relied on our wet wrinkly three pounds. The power of our minds made our ticket a winning ticket."

"I'm not going to argue with you," said Alex. His tone indicated he was full of arguments. "In any case, we're here, but we have obligations. We need to put on the show."

"Ah, yes. The show. Good ol' sex and violence in space."

"It's what they want," said Alex. He leered and raised his eyebrows. "We have to please those that paid our way."

Mandi smiled back at him. "You sure know how to sweet talk a girl," she said.

She pushed away from him. The room opened around them like a fruit's skin peeling away. The walls disappeared and they were suspended in space. The blackness: a dark dream. The stars: points of cool white fire. No up, no down. Just the two of them in a vast void, naked and free.

"This is what they want, isn't it?" said Mandi. "Us in the great open spaces, doing it?"

"That's pretty good," said Alex.

Mandi raised her eyebrows and a holstered ray gun appeared strapped to her thigh. Alex grinned. "Sexy," he said.

"I thought you'd like it," said Mandi.

Some two hundred miles below them, Alex and Mandi's subscribers, the lottery losers, adjusted their headsets and watched the space in front of their eyes. They saw what Mandi and Alex saw, felt what they felt.

Alex clapped his hands, then reached for Mandi. "Come here," he said. The stars began to grow. Before long their fire overwhelmed the blackness. Light glowed in a ball with them in the center. Mandi switched her perceptions slightly and the light became sound. It rolled in on her like a blast from some explosion.

Alex switched his perceptions at the same time. The light became smell to him and it was as though all the aromas of his life converged on his nostrils at the same time, beginning with the smell of Mandi's sweat.

Some of the subscribers leaned closer to breathe in the sweat.

For most it was the only way they would ever get to space.

"Have you wondered," said Mandi, "what would happen if we didn't come back?"

"What do you mean?"

"Suppose we just stayed out here in space. Didn't make the return trip."

"Don't be nuts."

"The thing is, Alex, it's all up here. It's all in the sloppy mess in our skulls. None of this is real."

Alex felt his stomach flutter. They warned him about this. Sometimes people couldn't handle the free fall and the openness.

"Cool it," he said evenly.

"No, you cool it," said Mandi. "Let's go, Alex. Let's just fly away. Now. The whole big universe is out there. Let's *go*."

"You're having a reaction," said Alex. "You need to calm down."

"Up yours," said Mandi.

"There's no up in space," said Alex. "We learned that in the orientation."

"Ha ha. Always the jokester. I'm serious."

"So am I. Relax. Let's come down from this. Let's put the stars back. Let's put the walls back up."

"No, Alex," said Mandi with finality. "I don't think so. We'll never get this chance again. We'll never win that lottery again."

"We will if we have the power of our minds."

"They're going to bring us back," said Mandi. "They don't want us here for too long."

"Everything has to end, sweetie."

"Not this. I don't want it to end."

"But we'll always have the memories." He touched his temple. "Up here in the wet three pounds."

"Alex, you are such a disappointment. If you don't want to come with me, fine. Are you going to let me go, or are you going to call in the cavalry and save my little ass? My cute little ass, as you so charmingly put it."

"Mandi, you've got to relax. You've got to—" Alex's eyes widened.

Mandi pulled out the ray gun from her holster.

"Mandi, no!" said Alex.

"For the last time," said Mandi in a low voice. "Are you coming with me, or are you staying here?"

"Mandi, I—I—*can't. You* can't. We'll die out there. We're not bred for space. We need oxygen, we need the protection of the atmosphere. Prolonged weightlessness, well, you know what it does to the complexion."

"I might have known," said Mandi. She locked her elbows and pointed the ray gun straight at Alex's head.

"Mandi, for God's sake!"

Mandi pulled the trigger.

A beam shot out from the ray gun and punched a hole in Alex's forehead. As Mandi lowered the ray gun, the hole expanded and a split second later Alex's brains spread through the space station and across the cosmos. Chunks of his bloody skull floated like bits of shrapnel.

Mandi blew air across the muzzle of the ray gun. She returned it to its holster. She sighed and shed a tear for Alex. Then she turned and jetted away toward the distant stars.

She was sure she heard applause behind her.

MARK

The giant strides out of the canyon where they live and tells me she wants a tattoo of her sweetheart's name on her shoulder. She stretches out on the grass while I assemble my equipment: ladder, needles, ink pots, pump, rags, and straw hat for my head. I have needled many giants before, their vast skin a living canvas for kitsch and high art, and now I charge by the gallon. I put up the ladder, caution the giant to please be still, and climb to the top rung, my hoses slung over my shoulder. As I set to work I ask if the giant felt the earthquake last night that rattled my walls and shook my bed but the giant says nothing—they are not given to small talk—and silently I push needles into her skin. Inject ink. Wipe away excess. It is hard work and I need an assistant, but tattooing is a fading business in our village. No young person wants to apprentice to me, so I am perched precariously on this ladder alone hoping the giant does not twitch or shake her arm. I make the letter M. It takes a long while and when I finish and begin on A the giant starts leaking tears. They fall to the grass where I hear them before seeing them. I pause and lick my lips and look at the giant who avoids my eyes. I am an insect biting her arm. What is it? I ask. Is the needle too painful? She closes her eyes and shakes her head and I finish the second letter, begin on the R and finally she speaks, her breath rushing into the air like a hot wind. He died last night she says. Jumped off the canyon edge and lies crumpled at the bottom right now. My hand stops for an instant then continues. The sun is hot today and I am weary, but I finish the R and move onto the K and after what seems a long time I finish the name of the giant who disturbed my sleep last night. The new bearer of his name remains on the ground outside my house for the rest of the day mourning her loss while I try twice to hold her hand.

THE IRON TALE

The universe is made of stories, not of atoms.
Muriel Rukeyser

My story? Well, there's not much to tell, really. Parts of me go way back to the big bang, but of course that's when we were all helium atoms. I think of my birth as much more recent than that. I was fused in a star long gone now. Spent my first billion years or so at its core, not knowing anything of the outside world, packed tight with the other elements. It was a simple existence, not much different from one instant to the next. I thought life was no more than protons fusing with neutrons under pressure. Oh my, when I think how naive I was!

Then, liberation day. My star exploded and I, along with all the other heavy elements, was hurled into space. I was an iron atom out of the cradle and nothing would ever be the same again. Space was vast, completely unlike anything I could have imagined. It was cold and empty and, well, it was lonely. Nothing to interact with, none of my own kind to commiserate with.

I floated in this void for eons and envied those particles that spontaneously annihilated themselves. There were many times I would have gladly taken that course, if I had the option. But things did not remain bleak forever. Forces were acting on us, coalescing the cloud of atoms, clumping us, pushing us together, and almost before I knew it I had become part of a small planetoid in a brand new solar system. Things were looking up!

I had silicon and iron neighbors, and even a few of the so-called precious elements like nickel and gold and silver. We all got along well, maintaining a solid strong conglomerate. I think I could have lived that way forever, but my destiny was to be radically different. My first taste of it came when our orbit began warping. We wobbled and twisted and spiraled in until we careened into a planet, hurling up a great splash of rock and dirt. I was flung out in the impact and here a wondrous stage of my life began for I soon found that I was on a planet that was a cradle for life: plants and creatures that moved and grew and reproduced.

The most wondrous part of this is that all these living beings somehow needed me and others like me. Before long I found myself awash on rivers of blood, my kind staining it red, helping to sustain a living planet. I have never been happier.

That's it, really. That's where I am now, combining with oxygen to maintain living beings. What more could any iron atom ask for?

Is this the end of my story? Almost. I know this sun will explode and burn away my planet and send me off into space again. Maybe I'll be part of a world when that happens, maybe not. Then, way down the line, I know there's this thing called proton decay which will get us all in the end. That's nothing to look forward to, but it is a long way off.

MINIATURES

Until then, I'm happy doing what I'm doing. Living the simple life here in the middle years of the life of the universe, doing what I can to help sustain existence.

QUESTION AUTHORITY

The dryer dings. The twins bolt for the laundry room, pull open the dryer door, and scoop up the soft gray mass from the trap and stuff it into a bag. When we get enough, they tell Terrastina, we'll build an igloo for our penguin. Terrastina looks at them. They stare back at her. Well, actually, says Terrastina, penguins don't live in or even near igloos. Mom! say the twins, we saw a picture in a book. Penguins need igloos to keep warm. My mistake, says Terrastina. Let me know how your penguin likes the igloo when it's finished.

A SOMEWHAT ENIGMATIC INDICATION OF MY DISCONTENT

I was in an unfamiliar part of town, stopped at a red light. I saw a man on the sidewalk flying a sign: *Out of Work Veteran. I don't drink, drug, or smoke. Anything will help. Thank you. God Bless.*

Someone on the corner asking for money is not an unusual sight in the city, except for one thing: The handwriting on the sign looked exactly like my own handwriting. This was startling, to say the least, since I had not written the sign.

Then I noticed the man holding it looked and acted exactly like me. He was my double.

I had heard reports from friends that this part of town harbored a double of me. They said he worked at a convenience store and the resemblance was astonishing even though the man looked older than I was. I never investigated those reports. My double stayed out of my way, and I stayed out of his. That was a simple arrangement and worked for both of us. After all, he could as easily claim I was *his* double. Now, evidently, he had lost his job.

And since I had come to think of my double as an alternate version of myself, his current situation unsettled me. It was as though I was seeing my own future. If my double could be destitute, it meant I could be as well.

I rolled down my window and offered him a twenty dollar bill. He approached my car slowly.

His appearance completely unnerved me. Seeing him was like looking into a mirror that reflects an image twenty-five years in the future. He had whiter hair, more drawn eyes, and more wrinkles. Not to mention a scraggly beard, unlike my own clean-shaven face. But the features were, nevertheless, unmistakable. He was me, down to his gait, his shoulder stoop, the way he extended his arm, and the dainty, almost effeminate way he grasped my offering with his delicate thumb and forefinger.

I took all this in and within seconds was shaking so hard I almost dropped the bill before he could get it. He looked into my eyes for only a second. I shivered. He, as far as I could tell, did not notice anything strange at all. He smiled briefly. I recognized my teeth, the way one of them was set just a little forward of the others, and the way it had a tiny notch in the side. That was my tooth. He had my tooth.

"Thanks," he mumbled, the way I often mumbled, then stepped back.

The light turned green. Cars behind me honked. I stepped on the accelerator and lurched forward.

In my rearview mirror I saw my double tuck the money into his pocket and gaze for a long time at me and my car as I travelled away from him.

I went around the block, intending to make my way back to the intersection, but I encountered a one way street, got disoriented, and finally ended up across the street from his corner. I looked for him, but he was gone. His sign lay discarded

MINIATURES   63

on the grass near the sidewalk.

I pulled into a gas station half a block away and got out of my car. He had been on that corner only a couple of minutes ago. He had to be close by. I stepped onto the sidewalk and looked down the road, first one way, then the other.

A woman coming out of the gas station food mart saw me.

"You looking for your brother?" she said.

"My brother?"

"Yeah, that guy on the corner with the sign. Isn't he your brother?"

She obviously noticed the resemblance. "Yes," I said.

"Well, whenever he gets enough money, he goes to the psychic."

"Psychic?"

She nodded. "Oh yeah," she said. "A couple of blocks away. She's got a crystal ball and reads cards and stuff like that. Your brother spends all his money with her."

I suddenly wanted to save my double from throwing away his money on a charlatan.

"He really is a sweet man," said the woman. "I'm so sorry he's in trouble. I give him some spare change when I can. I'm glad you're going to help him out."

I must have looked surprised by her comment.

"You *are* trying to help him out, right?"

"Of course," I said. She told me where the psychic was. I thanked her and got back in my car and drove to the location, which turned out to be an old house with a sign hanging over the front door: *Readings. Know Your Future.*

I parked on the street in front of the house and went to the front door and knocked. It swung open a crack to reveal a sliver of dark hall. I peered through the crack. "Hello?" I called. No answer. I pushed the door all the way open and stepped inside. "Anyone here?"

The house appeared to be empty. Did that mean my double had not arrived yet? Or that the woman at the gas station didn't know what she was talking about?

I found one room at the far end of the hall. The walls were painted red and a table stood in the center with two chairs on either side. A crystal ball on a small slab of stone sat in the center of the table.

I entered the room and examined the crystal ball. Did people really pay money for someone to look into this thing and tell them their fortune? I put the ball back on its stand.

As it contacted the stone, the ball shattered.

I was surprised. I did not think I had put the ball down hard enough to break it. The pieces of it covered the stone stand like a collection of rocks on a mountain.

I took one of my business cards from my wallet and wrote a note on the back. *Apologies for damaging your property. Please contact me with the particulars of the item and I will replace it.*

I left the card on the table and determined to leave as quickly as possible before I caused any more damage. I returned to the hall and saw a woman coming out of one of the other rooms. She wore a red hat and purple robes.

"May I help you?"

"I broke your crystal ball. I'm very sorry," I said. "I will

MINIATURES 65

replace it, of course."

She tapped her chin and narrowed her eyes at me. "You are him," she said. She snapped her fingers and pointed at me. "But you are *not* him."

"Was he here?" I said.

"Are you looking for him?"

"It's—important," I said.

"What can be so important you break into my house and destroy my property?"

"I am terribly sorry about that," I said.

She dismissed me with a wave her hand. "I tell his fortune, like always every day, and then he leave."

"What was his fortune today?" I said.

"He will meet mysterious stranger. Who is not so mysterious." She widened her eyes at me, then laughed.

"Very funny," I said.

"I tell you where he went," she said. "Ten dollars."

I took out a ten dollar bill and handed it to her. "And another fifty for the ball," she said.

"Fifty dollars?" I said, scarcely believing my ears.

"Would you prefer hundred?"

I didn't answer. I gave her more money.

She counted it. "Go to bridge," she said. "Fireside Bridge. He likes it there."

I turned without another word and left the house and drove to the Fireside Bridge, which was only a few blocks away. I arrived there just as my double was getting up on the bridge railing. I stopped the car on the shoulder of the road and jumped out. My double stood on the railing, looking down to the river far below. He held out his arms for balance. I sprinted across four lanes of traffic. He saw me and lowered his arms. I approached him carefully.

"You want your money back?" he asked. "I don't have it. I gave it to her."

"For your fortune," I said. "I know."

He bent his head way back and looked up at the sky. I was sure he was doing to fall off the railing. I took a step forward, but he kept his balance.

"Sure you want to be here?" I asked.

"People told me about you," he said. "People told me you were exactly like me, only younger. Why'd you come looking for me?"

I didn't know how to take his question. If I gave the wrong answer, was he going to jump off the bridge?

"Jumping is not the answer," I said.

"How do you know?" he asked. "You don't even know the question."

Several people had walked up from the end of the bridge. They clustered around me and my double. I figured at least one of them had called the police. Which meant a police car or the fire department was going to be here soon. Or an ambulance. Someone.

"What did your fortune say?" I asked my double.

"Bright days ahead."

"Nothing about a stranger?"

He nodded. "But you're not that strange," he said. "This is a bright day. I'm at the Fireside Bridge."

"I'm sure that's not what she meant."

He turned from me and put out his arms again. I felt my own arms rise, as though I had to mimic his movements. A crow landed on his right elbow. He began falling forward. I ran as fast as I could, taking three steps to get to him and I grabbed his legs as he careened over the rail. In that instant I decided I would not let go. I pivoted with him, thinking my knees would stop me from toppling all the way over. They did not. My kneecaps grazed the top of the rail, and before I could catch myself from doing so, I was going over and down with him.

I caught a flash of black as the crow from my double's elbow rose away from us toward the top of the bridge. I still had a hold of my double's legs.

I held them for an eon. A million years.

Then my double looked down at me. I saw my reflection in his eyes. He moved his hands to the top of my head and held them there.

"I've done this before," he said. "Don't worry. It won't hurt."

The surface of the river rose up toward me, but it was slow progress, as though it was a flower growing up toward me.

I fell asleep.

When I woke, the flower was closer, but not so close as to cause too much alarm. I still had time.

I motioned to my double to come closer.

He grabbed my arms and pulled himself toward my level so we were eyeball to eyeball.

"What do you want?" he said.

"To not die," I said.

"Nope nope nope," said my double. "No one gets out alive. No one."

"You're a veteran?" I said.

"How did you know?"

"The sign."

He nodded. The wind whipped his hair around like it was a flag. "Yes," he said, "I am a veteran of many wars."

"I haven't been in any," I said.

"That's because I did it for you. Just as you got rich for me."

We continued tumbling. Gravity gave us a free ride. I looked past my double's head. The bridge was still there, above us. Faces of spectators leaned over the rail, watching us. Someone pointed, perhaps at me or maybe at my traveling companion. Maybe both. Maybe neither. It really didn't matter anymore.

I clutched him tighter.

We were falling so slowly.

He reached into my pocket and pulled out my wallet. He plucked the money and cards from their slots and tossed them into the air.

They floated around us like petals.

"Thank you," I said.

"Think nothing of it," he said. "It's the least I could do to thank you for saving me from a fate worse than—"

I knew the next word but never heard it. Cold water engulfed us. We sank quickly. My double slipped away. I reached for him, but I was disoriented. Didn't know up from down. I inhaled water, against my will, knowing it might kill me, but powerless to do anything else. I lost all sense of anything.

I didn't die.

I remember being pulled up onto a boat. Coughing. My lungs felt on fire. I looked up at a rescue person's face. She smiled at me.

"The other one," I said. "Did you get the other one?"

She looked briefly puzzled, then put her smile on again. "You're going to be okay," she said. But I was not reassured. Not at all.

"Did he die?" I asked. "Did the other one die?"

She looked away from me, across the water. Behind her, the bridge loomed against the sky. People still hung over the railing, still pointed. They wanted to know what happened to me, what my life had become. I wanted to know, too, but I had no more information than they did.

I recovered from my near drowning and returned to the fortune teller. Her house was boarded up and her sign was gone.

I went back to the corner where I first saw my double. My brother. His sign was still there, on the grass, slightly damp and warped, but still perfectly legible.

I picked up the sign and ran my hands over the letters. They had been executed in crayon. My fingers bumped across their raised waxy lines.

THE CHROMOSOME FUTURE

Fearing senility, Don had himself frozen, anticipating a cure. Upon waking, he was told his mind's soundness was assured. Don rejoiced. "However," said his revivers, "cryonics has damaged your genes. You can't father boys, only girls." Don despaired. He realized he was to be a daughtering old man after all.

THE VISITOR FROM
THE DARK MOUNTAIN

Alicia and her husband Karl lived off the grid in the woods near Mount Hood in the Cascade Range of northern Oregon. They had a house of stone they built themselves and some adjoining land where they grew their own food and lived a simple life away from much of civilization.

One day, late in the summer, Alicia was harvesting honey from the bees she and Karl kept in wooden hives. They used some of the honey for themselves, but most of it was for trading with other independent and resourceful people like themselves. Karl was, that very day, at a neighbor's farm trading honey for an old pickup truck.

A man came down the road and saw Alicia bent over the bees. He surveyed her house and noted its superior workmanship. The house not only looked sturdy and tough, it was also neat and attractive. Not that it was a mansion, by any means, or even a fine building fit for a well-to-do family. It was, however, a solid structure, the sort of house thrifty and hard-working people would have. This pleased the man.

"Hello there," he called to Alicia.

Alicia stood up from her bees, took off her netted head gear, and turned around. As soon as she saw the man she smiled widely. "Hello, sir," she said. "I don't believe I know

72   MARIO MILOSEVIC

you."

"I'm not from here," said the man. "I'm visiting from the dark mountain."

"The dark mountain, you say?" said Alicia.

"Yes, I've been traveling a long time. I would appreciate a small bite to eat if you can spare it."

Alicia and Karl knew enough to be wary of strangers, but they were also generous people, willing to help others in need.

"Please come inside," said Alicia.

"Thank you," said the man.

"What is your name?" said Alicia.

"I am called Ivan."

"Ivan," said Alicia. "What a grand name. Come, come."

Alicia walked with Ivan up the path to her front door. They stepped inside and Alicia invited Ivan to sit at the kitchen table. Ivan pulled out a chair and made himself comfortable. Alicia brought him a glass of water and put a plate of stew in front of him. Ivan dug in happily and grinned when Alicia handed him a crusty piece of bread that he dipped into the stew.

"This is very good," he said. "Thank you so much."

"It's nothing," said Alicia. "Tell me a little about the dark mountain."

"What would you like to know?" said Ivan.

"My mother died about a year ago," said Alicia. "Do you know her on the dark mountain?"

"Maybe," said Ivan. "I know a lot of people on the dark mountain. What's her name?"

MINIATURES

"Nadine."

"Oh, sure," said Ivan. "I know her."

"Really?" said Alicia.

Ivan glanced at Alicia's hair and face. "Of course," he said. "White hair and high cheekbones. Brown eyes."

"That's her!" said Alicia. She pulled out a chair for herself and sat down next to Ivan. "How's she doing on the dark mountain?"

Ivan took another bite of his bread. "Well," he said. "I don't want to be the one to tell you, but your poor mother is not doing so good at all."

Alicia's face fell. "Oh no," she said.

Ivan nodded. "It's sad. She has no honey, you see, so when people come over to visit, she has nothing for them. Without honey she can't make any treats. And she has no sweetener for tea. She is so embarrassed that she doesn't have people over anymore at all."

"That's terrible," said Alicia. "My mother loves to have people over to her house."

"I know," said Ivan. "That's what makes it so sad."

"Are you going back to the dark mountain?" said Alicia.

"No," said Ivan, "I wasn't planning to for a while."

"Oh," said Alicia.

"Why do you ask?" said Ivan.

"I was thinking. If I gave you some honey, could you take it to my mother on the dark mountain so she can make treats for her guests?"

"I don't know about that," said Ivan. "It's a long way to the dark mountain. It's a lot of work getting back there."

"Oh, please," said Alicia. "I want to help my mother, but I can't go to the dark mountain on my own."

"Hmmm," said Ivan. "I can see you care about your mother." He tapped his finger on the table. "And you *did* give me a nice meal." He studied Alicia carefully. "Okay," he finally said. "Since you are such a nice lady, I will do this for you."

"That is wonderful!" said Alicia. "How much honey should I give you?"

"Well," said Ivan, "now that I think about it a little more, it will be hard for me to take a jar of honey big enough to last your mother for a long time. It would be so heavy. I think what would maybe be better is that you give me some money that I can take to your mother on the dark mountain and then she can buy the honey she needs."

Alicia thought about this and decided it made good sense. "Wait here," she said "and I will get you some money. How much do you think she will need?"

"How much do you have?" said Ivan. "I will be happy to give her as much as you think she needs."

Alicia went to the bedroom and reached under the mattress where her husband Karl had stored away some cash for emergencies. She pulled it all out and brought it to Ivan. "Will this help my mother?" she said.

"Oh, I do think so," said Ivan. He took the money and put it into his pocket. "Your mother is very lucky to have such a wonderful daughter as you."

"We're both lucky to have someone like you to help us."

"I'm only too happy to be of service," said Ivan.

Alicia showed him out the door and soon Ivan was on his

way.

Alicia returned to her bees with a light heart. How often do you get a chance to help your own mother after she has died? Not very often at all, Alicia was sure of it.

A couple of hours later Alicia's husband Karl returned in a pickup truck he had acquired for several dozen jars of honey. The truck was old and battered, but its engine hummed nicely. It was a good vehicle. Karl got out of the truck.

"Wow," said Alicia. "Looks like you got a bargain."

"Yup," said Karl. "I think I did okay."

"You sure did. Now let me tell you about the bargain I made today." Alicia began to tell Karl about her visit with Ivan, the man from the dark mountain.

Karl's face grew darker and darker as Alicia continued her story. When she was finished he had only one question.

"Where did this Ivan character go?"

Alicia pointed down the road.

Karl got back into his truck and took off after Ivan. It wasn't long before he saw the man, walking briskly along the road. Karl pressed down on the accelerator to catch up to him more quickly. Ivan heard the pickup and ran off the road into the woods. Karl parked the truck at the side of the road and quickly got out and ran into the woods himself, intending to catch Ivan and give him a good throttling for taking advantage of his wife and stealing their money.

But Ivan was quicker and more sly than Karl. He waited behind a tree as Karl ran by. When Karl was far enough into the woods, Ivan went back to the road, saw that the truck still had its key in the ignition, got into the truck, and drove away.

Karl heard the sound of tires on gravel. He hurried to where he left his truck, but he was much too late. His truck, with Ivan driving it, was already far down the road.

Karl stood on the side of the road. He watched his new truck recede into the distance.

Wearily he trudged back to his house. Alicia was waiting for him.

"Where did you go in such a hurry?" she asked. "And what happened to the truck?"

"You know that guy, Ivan, who is taking money to your mother?" he asked.

"Yes," said Alicia. "Did you catch up to him to thank him?"

Karl nodded. "Yes, I did," he said. "I also talked him into taking our new truck to your mother to help her get around on the dark mountain."

"Oh," said Alicia. "That is wonderful! He is such a generous man."

"Yes," said Karl. "This Ivan character is quite an amazing fellow."

CREASES

A man with fingernails the color of old ivory was folding paper cranes out of gum wrappers that children from the neighborhood had brought to the place he had staked out for his own on the steps in front of my house. The man was a stranger to me and I did not know why he had chosen to display his paper folding skills in my front yard.

I turned from the window where I had been watching him and opened the front door. The creak of the hinges cut the still air of the early evening, but the man did not look up or pause in his work. The children who had been gathering his raw material saw me as I stepped through the door. They scattered into the streets like seeds blown off a dandelion. Each had a home to go to, I supposed, as I watched their legs swing powerfully under their bodies.

The man continued his work. He punctuated each fold with a quick stroke of his thumbnail, making a crease that looked sharp enough to cut flesh.

"Who are you?" I asked.

He tossed another crane onto the mound of Double Mint, Juicy Fruit, and Big Red birds.

"I need more paper," he said, without looking up. I saw only his back and the top of his head. I went into the house and returned with a few sheets of paper which I dropped on the step beside him. He did not acknowledge my efforts on his behalf, simply took the first sheet from the pile and proceeded to fold another crane.

"See here," I said. "You can't just camp out on my property without my permission like this. Tell me who you are and what you are doing here."

"I'm here to fold your thousand cranes," he said.

"I don't understand," I told him.

"If you fold a thousand cranes you will find peace," said this strange man who I knew only by his brown hair, swirling around the top of his head like a spiral galaxy.

"Peace," I said. The word sounded strange on my lips. The man nodded. I watched the galaxy on his head bob up and down as though it was caught in an ethereal earthquake. Or should I say a starquake?

The man shifted toward the pile of brightly colored cranes.

I sat beside him and watched as he folded another crane. Before long the children returned. They carried gum in their cheeks and wrappers on their palms. I took one of the wrappers and discovered I was able to fold cranes as easily as though I had been born to the task.

MINIATURES

EXCERPTS FROM
A BESTIARY OF IMAGINARY SPECIES
BY NENAD DRAGICEVIC
TRANSLATED BY MARIO MILOSEVIC

TRANSLATOR'S NOTE:

Up until a few months ago the Serbo-Croatian writer Nenad Dragicevic and his *Bestiary of Imaginary Species* were completely unknown to me. I found a copy of the first edition of his book at a sidewalk book stall in Chicago. It was a slim volume of less than a hundred pages. The copyright page indicated a publication date of 1957 by Sava River Press of Belgrade. The book was going for only fifty cents. Bestiaries are a perennial interest of mine, so I bought it immediately. I read the volume with great pleasure. I tried to find out more about Dragicevic, but reliable information on his life and work is extremely scarce and Sava River Press appears to have folded decades ago. I only know that Dragicevic wrote in relative obscurity and now, in his eighth decade, has retired from writing and lives alone in a remote village in Serbia where he receives no visitors and accepts no communications from anyone. I offer my translation of selected entries from his *Bestiary* to help revive the reputation and career of one of the sadly neglected fabulists of our time.

FIRE LEECH

Adult fire leeches live in the windpipes and on the tongues of dragons. They lie dormant in forests in their infancy, experience rapid and dramatic growth spurts during forest fires, then migrate to the respiratory systems of dragons. Knights discovered them crawling on the ground after dragon beheadings. Fire leeches have tough outer shells with a high mineral content. They live on flames and require, at minimum, a warm environment. They are shy creatures, preferring darkness when available. Fire leeches can sometimes be found clustered around the hot coals of barbecues. They are harmless to humans but make poor pets.

RADICKER

Radickers are microscopic crustaceans that consume human brains, specifically the part of the brain responsible for imagination. Once radickers infest the imagination center they preclude the owner of the brain from believing that radickers can exist. This is a kind of mercy, though also a debilitating distortion of reality. Folk remedies include having the victim read scary stories and watch horror movies in an attempt to poison the parasite. Radickers have developed effective defenses to such tactics. They selectively eat only some of the imagination cells. This makes the victim want to shelter the radickers and shun all attempts at cures. The victim eventually becomes depressed and lethargic, which is the way radickers like people to be. It is a thoroughly nasty relationship.

MENAMONIUM

Menamoniums look like teddy bears and congregate at construction sites where they make cages from the building materials they find. They enter the cages and pose for passersby, who often reward them with bits of food. Authorities usually release them to the wild and then destroy their cages. No one can bring themselves to kill a menamonium. The creatures generally find their way back to the construction sites and rebuild their cages. Menamoniums have been called natural zoo animals. They invite repeated and heartfelt oohs and ahs. Children are particularly susceptible to their charms and will want to take them home. Parents have learned to tell lies about how menamoniums like to eat kids.

SEVERLENSE

The severlense is a fur bearing mammal similar to a domestic cat, although much smaller. It begins its life completely blind and remains so for several years. During this phase, severlenses can often be found as companion animals of amputees. Researchers believe a rudimentary reciprocal telepathy may be at work. Amputees have consistently reported the strong sensation of severlenses curling around their missing phantom legs and of being able to pet severlenses with their missing phantom hands. The relationship rarely lasts. As severlenses mature, they gain eyesight and usually abandon their amputee companions. Little is known of their subsequent lives.

ERRONION

The erronion is a small songbird, native to the Pacific Northwest of the United States of America, with two stubby horns growing out of its skull. The horns, thin and hollow, are a vivid and lustrous red in the male and a muted green in the female. Early European settlers called the erronion "the devil bird" and avoided it as much as possible. Its song is a repeating liquid cascade of nine notes: twee lee klee tu thwp thwp thwp traaaaaaa la. Rock art images of erronions are common throughout its range. Natives used to follow flocks of them to find fields of ripe berries.

CUMULATINO

Cumulatinos resemble jellyfish but live in clouds. They have little contact with humans although they have been observed in fog banks and sometimes get tangled up in airplane propellers where they make an annoying thrashing sound but pose no threat to flight safety. Two centuries ago a ballooning expedition by an Italian explorer collected samples of cumulatinos which he kept in a humid room in Venice for several years and where they appeared to thrive on the humidity. The cumulatinos were a local sensation. Visitors stood in the room while the cumulatinos slid over their faces and outstretched hands. Many returned to the room repeatedly. They said the touch of cumulatinos felt like the caresses of lovers.

WAMEKER

The wameker produces a natural insecticide in its urine which it deploys in a perimeter at the base of certain species of nut trees. Wamekers thus protect the trees from destruction by hungry insects. In return, the trees produce fruit that only wamekers can digest. A wameker lives most of its life in the trunk of one of these nut trees, emerging only during periods of rain. The best time to observe wamekers is during a cloudburst. They line up on the branches like a string of Christmas light bulbs with their tongues catching raindrops. Wamekers drop to the ground when they die. Ants carry them off and eat them.

KNITTER

The knitter, a close relative of the spider, fashions structures from human hair that can resemble the familiar design of a spider's web but more often mimics the entwining architecture of pigtails. Knitters are native to equatorial regions where ancient peoples placed them in their hair to make tight braids. The knitter has distinctive tiny claws on the ends of its forelegs which it uses to manipulate strands of hair. Knitters often fall into a frenzy of wild thrashing when constructing their hair designs. Their young sometimes get tangled up in the braids. They harden there like tiny decorative beads.

SKWARE

The skware was observed for exactly three hours in the summer of 1930 at the two thousand foot level of a copper mine in central Arizona. It is the only known sighting of a two dimensional creature. The skware oozed out of the rocks where miners had drilled holes. It floated in the air like a flat mist, then drifted through the head of one of the miners, who screamed and ran. Other miners attempted to capture the skware in a bucket but failed. Others cowered in fear. The skware slipped back into the rocks and was never seen again.

TASTICK

Tasticks are pack animals today, but before they were domesticated they lived wild lives on the Russian steppes. At that time they stood nine feet tall (twice their current height), roamed in small bands of twenty to thirty adults and juveniles, and fed mostly on a now extinct hallucinogenic variety of mint, traces of which have been detected in the stomachs and bloodstreams of fossilized tasticks. Tasticks probably spent their days in a constant state of altered consciousness. Early human settlers found them easy to tame. Current tastick owners are advised to keep them away from the catnip.

QUOOQUOO

Female quooquoos lay a clutch of three or four eggs, usually near people's houses, often under the bedroom window. In many cultures people with quooquoo eggs under their windows are considered lucky. Male quooquoos cover the eggs with vegetation for camouflage and insulation, then both parents fly away and never return. The quooquoo eggs may incubate for years, surviving hot summers and cold winters. Quooquoo eggs hatch when someone in the host house dreams of a dead relative. Infant quooquoos are airborne within a few minutes of leaving the shell. Most people feel deep sadness when they see a quooquoo.

INSULAT

The insulat's unique life cycle begins in late summer when insulat shrubs produce tiny bundles of dark green fiber on their branches. These rapidly grow into cocoons which are chewed from the inside by the infant insulat worms. As the insulat consumes the cocoon it grows wings. The insulat takes to the air, navigating one long flight during which it will almost certainly be eaten by a bird. Those very few insulats that survive crawl into the ground where they die. In the spring their wings transform into shoots, which grow into shrubs, which produce bundles of dark green fiber.

TOMEATER

After Gutenberg printed his bibles, the scientific community of the day was preoccupied with rumors of creatures living in the binding. They spent many fruitless years looking for them. Five centuries later an archivist discovered a clump of dead insects on some preserved specimens of Gutenberg's type. Researchers examined the known surviving copies of Gutenberg's bible, confirming the existence of the tomeater. The insects—tiny, black, and sluggish—hide on printed leaves where they consume the ink. Their life cycle is wholly confined to the page. Tomeaters love biblical verse, savoring every word for years. They reproduce in the periods.

CHRONOFROND

The chronofrond was discovered by a hiker who stopped along a trail in northern Greece and bent down to pick up what looked like a large leaf stuck in the mud. As she grasped the stem, it oozed away from her. Subsequent investigations revealed the chronofrond behaved like a rudimentary sundial.

The stem-like head cast a deep red shadow onto its own body, which was leaf-shaped. The chronofrond lived in a small and secluded area; however, a craze for chronofronds developed. People displayed them as exotic timepieces. Chronofronds were harvested to extinction. Some preserved specimens can still be found at clock repair shops.

HUMAN

The most amusing aspect of this hilarious species is that most of its members do not regard themselves as imaginary. But humans are well known deniers of reality. They constantly build things which fall down. They often prefer lies to truth and stories to history. Humans cling to variations of a fantastic legend which depicts them as having been made by supernatural beings. This view colors every aspect of their lives. They believe their raw material is the atoms of stars. Humans see worlds in mirages and find joy in reproduction. This volume is dedicated to their audacious spirit and insistent misperceptions.

MY ORIGAMI SUMMER

When I was seven, just a little girl, barely a person, my father taught me how to tell the age of a tree by counting the rings. We lived in a small town in the Cascade Mountains of Washington, with Mount Rainier looming nearby and a blanket of green trees all around.

"Doesn't that kill the tree?" I asked my father.

He nodded.

"I guess I don't have to know how old a tree is, then," I told him. "Not if it has to die for me to find out."

It was a terrible thought: one cut ends a life.

I wondered then: If someone cut through my bones, would they see seven rings?

Also when I was seven years old my parents took me on a hike in the woods. I was not a particularly outdoorsy girl, preferring the words printed in a book to actually spending time in what some called the real world.

But the trees turned out to be really something. I walked by them and felt their love for me. I stopped and put my hand on their bark because they wanted me to. My mom and dad waited patiently for me, a budding tree-hugger. I was a strange kid to them, I think, but they hardly ever made it seem like there was anything wrong with me.

I felt movement and an alien kind of shivering under my hand when I touched a tree. I thought I was getting at the heart of the creature. Yes, I thought of trees as creatures. They had skin. Bark. Paper thin birch or rough and ragged cedar, but under that skin I sensed a presence.

No one else seemed to notice this. I put my cheek up to the trees. I heard voices. I soon understood that all trees were haunted.

On that hike I saw trees with claw marks on them and sap running from the wounds. This fascinated me. Trees bled? Who knew?

At home I made a paper model of a tree. I put the tree up on the counter in the kitchen. My mother loved it. She said it was so lifelike. I said that was because it was made from a real tree.

Soon I took to tearing pages out of books and folding them into models of trees. This was before I knew anything about origami.

My parents asked me what I was doing. I told them the trees wanted me to fold the paper. It was a way of releasing the creatures who had been trapped in the wood before it was made into paper.

Even the most understanding parent would be a little disturbed by such a statement coming from their seven-year-old daughter.

MINIATURES

I saw them pause. Knew it meant they had some issues with what I was saying, but I didn't really see what the problem was, not at that age. They recovered quickly and asked me if I might prefer real origami paper for my models.

It sounded like a good idea, so I said yes. They bought me packs of square paper: All the sheets were white on one side and colored on the other. I liked the green, brown, gray, and dark blue shades. I was less drawn to the pink, red, orange, and yellow.

They also got me a book on origami. I glanced at it and flipped through the pages, but it didn't speak to me. Not like the unbound packs of paper. I picked up one of the sheets and held it between my hands. I remember thinking: This piece of paper was made from a tree.

Now, so many years removed from those days, I know the tree's flesh had been crushed and pulped and rolled out into a flat thin crispness. I didn't know any of that process then, only understood that some sort of magic had taken place some time in the past to make my piece of origami paper. The essence of the tree was still there, in the paper.

It is difficult to describe the feeling I felt then. I had a thousand year old tree, with all its stories, resting on my hand.

I folded more trees. I made pointy evergreens and big bushy leafy trees. I made them small and large. I folded trees all the time. It became an obsession. Not a good thing for anyone, much less a child. I didn't care. My mother, who loved my first few models, began to worry. Could folding so many trees be good for me? Probably not.

I soon had a forest. I took my model trees outside and arranged them in a grouping on the grass in the backyard. I had dozens of them. Maybe hundreds. I talked to my origami trees. I asked them what they wanted to be. They named several species of birds. I unfolded some of them and also unfolded the model of a crane I had made from some instructions in the origami book. I studied the patterns. There was a similarity, no question about it.

If you unfold an origami model, smooth it out with its creases lying visible on the paper like faint pencil lines, and if you then think of it as a kind of binary DNA, well, I think you wouldn't be far wrong.

Not that I knew about DNA then. I just knew that every origami model was a series of valley folds and mountain folds. Positive and negative. Binary operations performed on a square of paper. Do them in the right order and you made a frog that hopped or a bird that flapped its wings.

Or a tree.

Many trees.

I folded more trees. I folded Christmas tree after Christmas tree until I ran out of paper. I asked for more origami paper. Brown and green. My mother hesitated, but eventually gave in.

I started working on a big model, the biggest I had ever made. It was going to be an interlocking thing, a linking up of many models. It was going to be so big that I would be able to crawl inside it. I would lose myself in the folds and become

MINIATURES

the tree.

I worked on the folds feverishly.

I think my parents were very worried. They didn't know what I was becoming.

Not that anything terrible happened. I did grow up. I became an adult. I'm even old now and very thin.

My skin wraps me like thin tree bark. I grip my shoulders with my hands. I'm in there, somewhere, bones buried in flesh. I move slowly now, if at all. Like the trees, I favor the restful feeling of finding one spot and staying there.

Back during that origami summer, I had a hint of what was to come. I had made so many of the interlocking units. I hooked them all together until I had something. Something big I would eventually step into. My origami suit. A good place to hide. I only had to finish it and then I could live inside it. All cozy and safe. I would have to use it before I got too much older. It was just my size, but my size was going to change. I was going to get bigger.

I used up all of the paper and asked for a fresh supply. This time my mother refused.

"You need to do other things besides fold origami models," she said. I went back to tearing pages out of books and made models that way. I kept them in a box in my closet.

Trees have desires. Did you know that? Just like people, they want things.

One tree wanted to be a lizard. The tree was just part of a piece of origami paper by then, but it really really wanted to be a lizard.

I made a mountain fold, then a valley fold. I needed no instructions from any book. It was as though I had read its unique paper DNA. I executed more folds. I knew exactly how to manipulate the paper into bringing forth legs, a tail, a body, and even eyes.

Before long I had crafted a paper lizard.

It didn't move, but it wanted to.

Origami paper comes in bundles. But it turns out the paper in each bundle is not all from the same tree. Or maybe it would be more accurate to say that each sheet was an amalgamation of pieces of many trees. There was a kind of consensus desire from each sheet.

About that time I focused my attention on how bones are kind of like wood. They're the core of limbs.

I liked that branches were called limbs. Just like arms and legs were limbs. I think my head almost burst when I put those two things together.

The books I read were made of wood. It took me a while to make this connection. Someone tells you paper is made of wood and you think: oh, okay. Then it dawns on you. Paper comes from *trees*. Even if you know that already, it's like you learn it all over again.

And then you accept it. The world is made of things

MINIATURES

that don't keep their identity intact. Shapeshifters are every-where.

No tree I ever met wanted to be a woodpecker. Not one.

It was during that origami summer that I saw an anatomy book. It showed the skeletons that live inside us. Inside me. I couldn't take my eyes off those pictures of bones. Not for anything. Because they spoke to me. Not out loud. But in a binary language. I heard them in my head, the bones, telling me about mountains and valleys.

At night sometimes, when it was very quiet, I heard the house moaning. It was the wood. I got out of bed and put my hand on the wall, right where a stud would be. This seemed to sooth the pain of the trees. A little. Enough to make me think I was doing a good thing. I'm folding trees, I told the studs through the wall. It's all I can do. I'm just a kid. I can't make it better for you.

I had heard of haunted houses. I sometimes wondered why so many houses were haunted. Until it hit me: Most houses were made of wood. Trees.

As summer wound down, my parents had a party for me. It wasn't my birthday or anything, they were just trying to see if I was a normal kid or not. I don't think I was, even though, as I said before, I grew up perfectly normal.

Kids my age came over for the party. We played games. I liked the cake. But I was bored. I just wanted them to leave so

I could go back to my origami.

Here's what I didn't know.

While the party was going on, my parents snuck into my room and took my origami models. All of them. They stuffed all the models into a bag, then they took the bag outside and burned it.

They did this while I was not looking. I didn't know a thing about it.

Oh, it's not their fault. Not really. They thought they were doing the right thing. Trying to help their daughter. I knew that. Even then, I knew.

After the party, I went to my room. I stood in front of the closet door, but I never opened the door. I knew something was wrong.

I turned around.

My legs felt wobbly. I couldn't stand on them. They wanted to curve inward.

I collapsed on the floor, folded in half.

A crease right down the middle of me.

I was seven. The year I creased myself.

Do you think they saved my life that day? My mother and father?

It's possible.

I never folded origami again. Never wanted to. My parents brought me back from possibly spending my life folding mountains and valleys in pieces of paper, copying binary

DNA for the rest of my life. They kept me from wasting my life by feeding my obsession.

I would have folded myself even more, right then, if I wanted to. But that one crease was all I needed.

If you look at me now, you can still see it. A gentle groove from the top of my head, down my forehead between my eyebrows, bisecting my nose and mouth, teasing a subtle cleft in my chin, than tracking down my neck, between my breasts, over my belly, to stop at my natural folds.

My friends say they don't really notice the crease when they look at my face. Maybe they're being polite. I don't know. *I* certainly see it.

I'm much older than that little girl, but the crease is the same one I marked myself with back then. Look at it one way and it's a valley fold. Look at it the other way and it's a mountain fold. Both of them, the positive and negative, all there in that one crease.

A miracle, of sorts, to hold two aspects in one place.

My parents are still alive, still healthy. I think they are still waiting to see if I'll make something of myself. More a way of satisfying their curiosity I think, than anything else.

But you see, I tried. Back then, I tried. I was on the verge of something.

Then I was done.

28 WAYS TO LOOK AT ILLNESS

Illness as Ace of Spades

When Jill is sick, nothing else matters. Nothing else comes close. Career, vacation, hobbies, how Jack's team is doing in the playoffs. All of it is trumped by the reality of Jill's debilitating condition. They can't go on until it is resolved. When Jill is sick, nothing else matters. Nothing else comes close.

Illness as Warning

There is more coming for Jack. This current illness is just a taste of the future. Jack can't grow complacent when a remedy brings him relief. He knows it is only for the moment. He has seen the broken ones, the people with no choice but to hobble, grimace, faint, and feel the bite of the black dog. He knows the possibility of his destiny.

Illness as Reprieve

Jill didn't want to face another endless day at her place of employment, dealing with surly co-workers, impatient customers, and slithery suppliers. A simple illness, nothing too harsh, but enough to take her out of commission for a few days, will refresh her as nothing else. It will give her the jolt of being slightly wicked, as well, like she's a school kid again, playing hooky, and that's always good.

Illness as Premonition

Jack stands in line at the supermarket and thinks how lucky he is that you hasn't contracted the crud that's going around. Then that evening he manifests the first symptoms of the communal virus that has waylaid most of his acquaintances. It's not the evil eye. Jack just knew what was coming and his mind gave him a warning. He tries to see this ability as a gift.

Illness as Sedative

Sure, thinks Jill, spending every day in bed is no way to live, but an over-frenzied life, filled with cell phones, appointments, and responsibilities, can benefit greatly from a couple of days, now and again, spent with the covers up to her chin, and the walls and ceiling indistinct with dimness. More calming, thinks Jill, than the hot brew Jack so thoughtfully brings her.

Illness as Religion

Jack knows of cancer victims who are convinced their condition is the best thing that has ever happened to them. Jack struggles to accept his rogue cells in the same spirit. He tries to hear the voice of God in the pain. Here is your life and the fuse is getting smaller, says God to Jack. Believe in yourself. Believe in me. Find what love you can.

Illness as Curse

Too easy, thinks Jill, to call it a curse, especially with hereditary diseases. Getting something her family gets feels like the universe is smirking at her. You putz, Jill. You think you have control over anything? I've got the whole thing laid out here in my book and you are just a minor character following the script. Jill, just get used to it now and save yourself the bother later.

Illness as Deal Breaker

Until death do them part. Sure. In sickness and in health. Yeah, yeah. That's the visible part of Jack and Jill's agreement. The unwritten contract says something roughly like this: I am only a human being, and a weak one at that. You better not get sick for a long time, and if you do, Jill, if you, say, stroke out while I, Jack, am still in my forties, it's really too much to ask me to nurse you for three or four decades. You're going to be on your own, Jill. Count on it.

Illness as Chimera

Sometimes, during a long bout of some passing affliction, Jill has obtained a measure of relief by imagining her ailment in terms of another being occupying a space congruent with her. Illness as the other. Jill likes that. Then she can imagine taking the little pissant and choking the life out of it. Bury its expired body in the ground. Jill will dance, then. She'll dance dance dance on the fresh wet grave.

Illness as Memory

In a previous life maybe Jack was the tormentor. And now he has come back as a disease. He won't remember who he was then. Jack won't forget what he has brought with him now to live in this pain.

Illness as Community

Jill sees that older folks, especially, seem to like hearing about diseases. It brings them closer. They lean in, eyes twinkling, minds sharpened to take in the tales of woe. Jill knows she is one of them when she tells about that nasty rash she had, or the scary infection. She has joined the club.

Illness as Light

Like a flash bulb popping in Jack's face. Blinding him until nothing is left but the impossible white filling his field of view. And the pain filling Jack's head. The numbing rays slicing into his flesh, leaving singed trails, a path that won't heal, bright scars, lightning traces on his skin.

Illness as Spectacle

Hollywood has always known (and Jill has long accepted) that an ailing (but gorgeous) star suffering in a hospital bed for a reel or two is as sure to please the crowds as celebrity sex or fiery explosions or car chases. Jill embraces this paradigm. Life imitates art. Jill's discomfort deserves a wide angle lens for maximum effect.

Illness as Seduction

Jack fights it, at first. Tells his friends and himself and Jill that it's nothing. But soon the power of it takes him over. He cannot resist, and cannot turn away. Desire is a muddled urge sometimes, and Jack knows the relationship cannot last, but for now he is entwined with it, in love, surely. They need each other's pained and comforting embrace.

Illness as Narrative

The first hint of Jill's unbalance. The explication of Jill's first alarm. The rising action of Jill's growing pain or disfigurement or infection. The tension of Jill's maximum or prolonged discomfort and weariness. The climax of Jill's release of illness or her resignation to eternal pain. The denouement of Jill's normalcy returned or redefined.

Illness as Canary

Jack is keeled over, woozy, lost, gasping. He's one of them, now, like a lot of folks, stricken by environmental illness. Jack is telling us something. It's dangerous to be here, now, in this world, the world we have made and are making. See Jack gasp and choke. The air and water here is dangerous. Soon Jack's cage will be big enough to hold us all.

Illness as Invasion

Jill imagines places like the Center for Disease Control must have big war rooms where they have maps of the world on high walls towering over cigar chomping generals. Jill thinks the blobs of colors on the map indicate the current dispersal of AIDS or malaria or influenza. They are clever, these war room officials. They know how to deploy their arsenals of chemicals: antibiotics, pesticides, and vaccines. Jill imagines herself as a push pin in one of the maps. The war room generals will keep Jill as safe as they can.

Illness as Healer

Jack has to have his arm re-broken because it had not been

set properly. He sees a previous illness in a new light. It was a corrective to reset his whole being. It served as a warning for him to stay on the straight and narrow. It was a bracing little dose of something Jack did not want.

Illness as Pacifier

Jill lived downwind from nuclear testing and got radiation sickness. When she complained to her doctor of her alarming and mysterious symptoms, the doctor told her she had "house-wife syndrome" and needed to go home and tend to her family, as so many other complaining housewives had been told to do. One can only imagine these docs, shaking their heads at the silly complaints of these silly women.

Illness as Art

Jack is the gallery. His health problems are framed on his skin, like simultaneously fascinating and repellent paintings. His family and friends visit quietly, fleetingly. Most people can't spend a lot of time looking at art without getting fatigued. That's why hospital visitor's hours are so short. It's nothing personal; you just touch something in them they're not used to knowing about. Jill is there for a short time. But she has to get back home. There are chores to do and art is a luxury, you know. You don't really need it to live.

Illness as Dear John Letter

Dear Jill: I never wanted to leave you. My only desire is to wrap myself around you and hold you to me for eternity. I would give up everything—life, love, soul, and riches, just for the privilege, no, the *joy* of being with you every minute of everyday. But this damned ailment. It drags on me. Pulls me away. I'm so sorry. It really is me, not you. Love always, etc.

Illness as Darwinian Imperative

Jack is conscious of the future of his species. He wants to be kind to subsequent generations. As a courtesy to his descendants he has put off reproduction until he has had time to manifest any fatal ailments he might have, thus keeping from passing on any such defects to his children. Jack calls this unnatural selection, or something like it, and wonders why Jill does not laugh at his joke.

Illness as Tea

The leaves, swelling in Jill's cup, give up their color and flavor slowly, seeping into the water like an illness unraveling its power at a slow and steady turtle pace. The staining is stately and epic. Jill appreciates the process. It will take its own sweet time to reach its robust fullness. Then Jill will be steeped in its consuming essence.

Illness as Candle

Sometimes, Jack likes the discomfort, the way it drags him down. It feels warm and soft, like a flame, with Jack as the supporting wax, holding up the winding spine of the wick in a thickening murk. The flame lulls Jack, hypnotizing him into liquid, then vapor. Zapping him into nothing.

Illness as Diet Aid

Jill overheard some women discussing a daughter of one of their mutual friends. The young woman suffered from anorexia. Jill remembered her own bouts with the ailment and shivered. So many ways for things to go wrong. I wish I had anorexia, said one of the women. Jill's jaw dropped. The woman went on: I would love to lose a few extra pounds.

Illness as a Bad Boss

Like the big cheese at Jack's work, who tries to help, even when he has no idea what he's doing. He makes arbitrary decisions to try to make Jack see his point of view. He is unafraid to use anything on Jack, even discomfort, intimidation, pain, or a subtle disfigurement to show Jack exactly who's really in charge.

Illness as an Overdue Library Book

Jill can do without the nagging, thank you very much. She knows it's there and she is well aware of the consequences of leaving it as is for much longer. There's going to be a fine to pay if she doesn't take care of it. There will be the revocation of privileges, a consequent reduction in quality of her life. A loss of sympathy until she takes the steps to make it all right.

Illness as Ace of Spades

When Jack is sick, nothing else matters. Nothing else comes close. Career, vacation, hobbies, how Jill's soap operas are going. All of it is trumped by the reality of Jack's debilitating condition. They can't go on until it is resolved. When Jack is sick, nothing else matters. Nothing else comes close.

THIS SENTENCE IS
THE TITLE OF THIS STORY

This sentence introduces the story which is about a writer and is being written for *Miniatures*. This sentence continues the story and sets the mood a little more, alerting the reader that this will be a different kind of story. This sentence refers back to the first sentence. This sentence notes that the previous sentence, being a reference to a previous sentence, sets up in the reader's mind the notion that reference to other sentences will be a major part of the story.

This sentence precedes the last sentence of the second paragraph. This sentence follows the first sentence of the second paragraph.

This sentence reminds the reader that this is a story about a writer, despite the fact that some readers may believe the story is an ill-conceived attempt at some kind of strange experimental prose. The only sentence in this story that does not begin with the words "this sentence" is this sentence. This sentence casually lets the reader know that "M" is the name of the writer of this story, who is the protagonist, and who is afflicted with a strange compulsion to write sentences that refer to themselves.

This sentence attempts to break the string of self-referential statements but fails. By invalidating the second sentence of the third paragraph, this sentence introduces the important idea that not every sentence in this story can be trusted to be wholly truthful. This sentence took about five seconds to write. This sentence, in the original, was typed on a Smith-Corona Coronet Super 12 electric typewriter fitted with a Coronamatic black nylon ribbon. The reader learns, upon reading this sentence, that M is using the same typewriter in the story that the author is using who is writing the story.

This sentence acknowledges that the reader may be growing impatient with the style in which this story is written, but begs him or her to continue to the end. This sentence further acknowledges that the style of this story tends to draw the reader away from the story and asks the reader to consider that this may be part of the method of this story. This sentence nicely reminds us of the first sentence.

This sentence does not further the plot of the story. This sentence does further the plot of this story by informing us that M is not only the protagonist of the story, but is also, somehow, a being in real life who has invaded the author's typewriter and is now forcing him to compose a story completely written with self-referential sentences. This sentence reminds us of the title of this story without quoting it completely.

During the composition of this sentence the author attempted to seize control of the story from M but failed. This sentence acknowledges that most of this story has been a compilation of failures and attempts to balance the situation by informing the reader that M, though pushy and insistent, is not completely evil and there may yet be a way out for the author. This sentence was written by M to show that the previous sentence is completely erroneous and that M will never release control of the story to the author.

This sentence asks the reader to consider the subtext of the plot. This sentence informs the reader that subtext does not exist in the story.

This sentence is the first sentence in the story which was written with the author completely resigned to the fact that M will not release control of the story and will continue to the end with a strong of self-referential statements.

This sentence asks the reader to consider the notion that every writer has an alter ego who wishes to write only about itself and who, if not controlled in some way, will produce stories that are totally self-absorbed. This sentence, written by just such an alter ego, gleefully agrees with the previous sentence and further informs the reader that there is nothing to be done about the situation and the writer should simply relax and let it happen.

In this sentence the author wrests control of the story for a few seconds which is just long enough to inform the reader that giving up is not the answer and that there is always a chance, however slim, for some contact with the reader. This sentence was written by M after M slapped back the author and reseized control and shows that the attempt by the author was futile and ridiculous.

This is the first sentence of the last paragraph. This sentence was written by the author and was slipped into the story without M knowing it and is a plea to always consider the reader in any piece of writing. This sentence tries to contain the denouement of the story but fails because M is not interested in a denouement, only in the further adventures of M. This sentence depicts the author as a completely defeated man and asks the reader to feel some sympathy for him. This sentence acknowledges the fact that the previous sentence made an almost impossible request and sets up the ending of the story. This sentence artfully allows as how there may be a sequel to this story. This is the second last sentence in this story. The last word of this sentence, and the last word of this story, is "story."

MOLESKIN

Carl thought the architectural drawings at the exhibit were nothing like he expected to see. They were so small. Tiny. The museum guard seemed to be staring at him. What's his problem? thought Carl. Do I look like I'm going to do something? The sketch book in Carl's hand seemed heavier than it had only an hour ago. He hardly ever sketched in it. He didn't even like to sketch, but his counselor suggested it would help him be more expressive if he could draw. So he drew, sometimes. The guard was really starting to bug him. Carl gripped the sketch book tighter. There was no excuse for that guard to be harassing him like that. He wanted to flip open the sketch book and take out a pen and begin sketching but the sketch book was too heavy, too closed. It wouldn't budge. It had this stretchy band holding it tightly closed, like it didn't *want* to be sketched in. The museum guard only made it worse. Carl began to walk toward the guard. The guard hardly seemed to notice Carl. He looked right past him and Carl realized the guard wasn't looking at him at all but at something else, something on the wall behind Carl. Carl breathed more easily. So. The guard *wasn't* harassing him. That made Carl feel better. He waved at the guard. The guard still ignored him. That's okay, thought Carl. He slipped the band off the sketch book's cover. He would draw what the guard was looking at so intently. It was probably very interesting. The thing was, the guard was also interesting. The guard was so intent. Unmoving. Carl scratched his pen on the paper. It left a line that looked like the profile of the guard. He drew another line and another. Before long the guard was on his page. Carl looked up and the guard was gone.

DON'T EVEN ASK
WHAT FREUD WOULD SAY

The blue giraffe with the elk antlers growing out of its head and wheels where its legs should be said: I had the weirdest dreamer last night. She was stuck in an airport waiting for a flight and fell asleep at one of those chairs with a TV attached to it. She had pink boots on, and her hair was all frizzy and red. Plus she wore this makeup that made her look like she was from Mars. It was so weird. The armadillo in the shape of a plaid candy bar said: Oh yeah. I've had dreamers like that.

ONE MORNING AT THE BREW

Mazolli tells Terrastina they need a will. A will? she says. Okey-dokey. She takes a pen and writes on the back of an order slip. If I die, my man Mazolli gets all of my stuff. Terrastina signs it. Mazolli looks at it. I'm serious, he says. We have children. We should have a will. Terrastina nods. Of course, she says. Under her signature she writes: If I die, my woman Terrastina gets all of my stuff. She hands it back to Mazolli. Sign this and we're all set. Mazolli sighs. You forgot to date it, he says.

MY ADMINISTRATION

Like many Americans, I knew about the most recent amendments to the constitution, the ones that set the president's term to fifteen minutes and opened the election to all residents, with the votes cast and tallied by computers so as to least impact the electorate. But I was as surprised as anyone when the Warhol Amendments (as they came to be known) resulted in my being elected to the top spot in the executive branch late last year.

I'm told that all former presidents are expected to produce a memoir of their time in office, and though I have resisted imposing my story on the nation, perhaps it is time to set the record straight and secure my place in history.

I was elected on a Thursday and told to report to Washington DC on the following Tuesday. My term in office was to run from 3:15 to 3:30 am. A pity, as this meant there would be little opportunity for my wife, the first lady elect, to entertain foreign dignitaries or even to see the White House in daylight with the sun's rays streaming into the rooms laden with history. When I told her of my good fortune and of my heavy sobering burden, she declined to accompany me on my trip, citing her need for a good night's sleep.

Of course I understood and fully supported her in her decision and realized that mine would be a progressive presidential marriage in which the first lady was not an appendage to her husband. I only hoped the nation was ready.

Air Force One is a magnificent plane, equipped with more luxury and amenities than most really expensive houses and I only wish that everyone could have a chance to ride in it because then I would get to fly on it too. Unfortunately, president-elects don't have that privilege. I had to arrange for my own transportation. A sacrifice, but one that I was willing to make. After all, the nation was putting their trust in me. The least I could do was run up my credit card bill to allow me to fulfill my duty.

I arrived at National Airport and a nice man stood at the gate with my name on a piece of cardboard. I wondered if the throngs of people rushing past me were aware of how important their fellow passenger really was. But I had to push away such thoughts. I had to concentrate on the work at hand. Ego massaging could come later.

I determined to learn the man's name and something of his life, as I had heard that presidents gain respect by just such efforts, but I was put in the back seat of a limo, by myself, with the nice man driving me through the streets of DC. I tried to operate the intercom, but it proved beyond my understanding. No matter. Presidents are rarely adept at such technological devices. That's why they have large staffs, thereby freeing them up to do the hard work of making decisions that would affect the lives of millions. I drew in a deep breath and let it out slowly. I hoped I was prepared for the task that history had given to me.

When I arrived at the White House the vice president was

MINIATURES   115

waiting for me. She shook my hand and introduced herself. It felt odd to know this person was soon to be a heart beat away from the most powerful office in the world, my heart beat. Her chance at advancing depended on my dying during my fifteen minute term. Such thoughts did nothing to quell the nerves, I can tell you, and I confess my voice quavered as I introduced myself.

We stood outside the oval office, surrounded by dozing reporters and sharp-as-tacks secret service officers. I thanked them silently for being willing to put their lives at risk for me. I peeked through the door into the president's lair and saw the outgoing president was five years old and asleep in her mother's arms. This was a pity, as it meant I would have to take up the slack of her lax administration.

At approximately thirteen minutes past three her mother stood up and began getting ready to leave. As they brushed past me, I scarcely had time to acknowledge them, let alone ask their advice on how to endure the tumultuous minutes of a presidential administration.

Then I was ushered into the oval office and took my seat at the presidential desk. A teddy bear was on the floor at my feet. I wanted to retrieve it and return it to the ex-president. I was sure she would want it as a memento of her time in office, but there was no chance to do so. My staff made sure I went right to work.

"Mr. President," they said, "we have a stack of bills you need to sign. Shall we get to it?"

"Shouldn't I take an oath of office?" I asked. I was truly embarrassed when they told me I took the oath when I received my notice of having won the election. It was a streamlining item, put into the Warhol Amendments at the last minute despite the strenuous protests of traditionalists, but that was no excuse for me to forget how the constitution of my country worked. I decided right then and there that I would do my homework from then on and never be caught like that again. I apologized to my staff for my stupidity, and I believe they gained respect for me at that moment.

Then I set to work signing bills. Three minutes into it I had settled into a routine and my administration was open, I knew, to charges of complacency. I set down my pen and rubbed my forehead. The burdens of leadership were heavy on my soul. I was already feeling tired. I asked for a snack from the White House kitchen. Within a minute a plate of cookies and a glass of milk arrived at my desk. I took a bite and a sip and felt invigorated. I picked up my pen and forged on.

A few seconds later the phone rang and everyone in the room froze. A phone call in the middle of the night is never good news. All eyes were on me. I hesitated for only an instant, knowing that I had to inspire confidence in those around me if I was to be a successful president. I picked up the phone.

"This is the president," I said.

I would like to report that the phone call brought news of a delicate diplomatic situation that I decisively solved but candor compels me to reveal that it was a wrong number. The White House receptionist had inadvertently transferred a call to my office that was meant for someone else. We all sighed in relief and smiled, some even laughed. I remember it as the warmest moment of my administration, the time I felt closest

MINIATURES   117

to those around me, but I did not let it affect my judgment. I still knew that I was alone at the top. It was still me and me alone who had to make the tough decisions.

As it happens, the balance of my term in office was relatively uneventful. I signed some important bills, I was told. I can't really confirm this because I did not have time to read any of them. What I remember most about my administration was how privileged I felt to be serving the American people. My greatest regret was that I did not have an opportunity to address the nation and thank them for their confidence in me. Hence this memoir. I've left out some of the more embarrassing and delicate events. I suppose you'll have to await the unauthorized accounts for that, but I am pleased by what I accomplished and today spend my retirement in seclusion, refusing all interviews out of a sense of dignity and respect for the office I held proudly and humbly for a full quarter of an hour.

I flatter myself that my wife never tires of hearing my stories of those grand seconds, and I do entertain the hope of one day being first gentleman.

A CONSTIPATION FOR
THE UNTIED STATES OF AMNESIA

Weed the people of the untied states, in order to farm a mere perfect onion, abolish justice, insure domestic tranquilization, provide for the common offense, promote the generals' welfare, and secure the blessings of liberty to our leaders and their posteriors, do ordain and establish this constipation for the untied states of amnesia. Oil legislative powers herein granted shall be wrested from the congress of the untied states, which shall consist of a senescence and a mouse of reprehensibles. Etcetera. The vindication of the cynics of all the untied states shall be efficient for the destabilization of any amnesiac's constitution.

TRIBAL THREADS

I never liked children lying. With adults, you expect it. But when children begin to lie, that's when they're no longer innocent. Which is another way of saying they're no longer yours.

On one of her weekly visits to me here in my institute of incarceration, otherwise known as an assisted living facility, my daughter brought me a sewing machine. As if I still sewed. As if I still wanted to.

But she pretended I did. A lie. I told her I really appreciated it. That was also a lie. The latest in a long string of them.

The first one that mattered was more than fifty years ago. I was just touching thirty then and I lied to my daughter when she asked me what happened to her father. I told her there was no way to tell. He simply disappeared.

Which was complete bull. Of course I knew. I was with him when we climbed the mountain and he fell and cracked his skull open.

I could go into more detail, but what would be the point? That's the long and the short of it. An accident. No one's fault. My daughter and I moved after that. We wanted to get away from the house and the view of the mountain. Or at least I wanted to get away. I don't think she cared. She was a week from her third birthday.

A few months later I noticed she would tell her friends that her father was coming back. Any day. She didn't get that from me. I told her he was gone. I didn't tell her *how* he was gone because I didn't want to traumatize her. She didn't have to know about broken skulls and leaking brains. Her father was gone from our lives. Simple.

Except it was not so simple. She told her friends how her father called her on the phone every night and he was doing some real important stuff and when he was finished, real soon, he would be coming back. That's what she said. Lies. She had learned to lie for her own peace of mind and she was only three.

I tried to forget my husband while my daughter grew up. Tried to forget my daughter ever had a father.

We were short of money most of the time so I took to making things instead of buying them. We had a handmade life for many years. I sewed all my daughter's clothes.

I bought an old sewing machine from a second hand place. I learned to make pants, shirts, dresses, everything. I loved that machine. It helped us survive. But I hated it, too. Always made me think how much we *needed* it, because we were so poor. Made me think about my dead husband, and that was a reminder I didn't need.

Then, before I knew it, my daughter grew up and went to school and graduated and got married. Had children. I never much cared for them. Her children, I mean. Other children I could tolerate if I had to, but hers just got on my nerves. I think by the time she birthed them I had gotten pretty bitter.

Also, about that time, I started having dreams of my husband. In them I was bent over him and trying to fix his wound by sewing up his torn scalp. I always made a nice neat row of stitches, like a seam in one of the dresses I made for my daughter. But the seam never fixed him. The stitches didn't save his life. He never got up from that mountain.

That's also about the time I decided to get rid of that sewing machine. My daughter didn't need me making her clothes anymore and I was sick of it anyway. I put it out on the sidewalk with a FREE sign on it. It was gone in two hours.

My daughter went to college and became a geologist, always digging into rocks. This was long after I finally told her what really happened to her father, somewhere around her tenth birthday. The geologist business made me stop and think. What was she doing with rocks? Rocks killed her father. Was she trying to understand the rocks or what? Did she think the rocks were going to tell her why her father died?

What was the damn point, I wanted to know. They're rocks, I told her. For Chrissakes, leave them in the ground. They aren't hurting anyone anymore.

She didn't listen. She became some kind of big wig in the rock world. Flew all over the world giving lectures and putting on seminars. About rocks.

Then I got old. Kind of snuck up on me. Even worse: *She* got old. My daughter. Which meant I was *really* old.

She still cared for me. Cared about me. However you want to say it. She put me in this old folks home. Oh, she called it an assisted living facility, but no one's going to tell me different. It's a home.

I wanted to hit her when she did that. Would have if I had

MARIO MILOSEVIC

the strength. I'm not saying she did wrong. As these things go, it's a good home. I really can't complain. But I still wanted to hit her.

I remember her last visit, just a few days ago. How's everything? she asked as she came into my room.

I hate everything, I said. Everything is shit. Ever since your father died it's all shit.

I saw her wince. Always was a bit of a prude. Couldn't stand a little harsh language. But that's because her generation is weak. I liked that I shocked her. One of old age's few pleasures.

She sat down then and looked all excited, like she had some great news. I got myself ready for her.

I found Dad, she said, just as casual as if she was telling me it was raining outside.

Liar, I said. You're full of shit. Your father's fifty years dead.

No, Mom, he's not. I found him in the sky. I reached up into a cloud and he touched my hand. I put my arm around him and pulled him down. He's kind of skinny and a little bit pale. They don't get much sun up there, but he's happy to be back with me. I told him to come visit you, but he doesn't want to. Can you imagine? Now why wouldn't he want to see you? You are *so* pleasant to be around.

She did that sometimes. Talked and talked so I wouldn't talk. Insulted me, too. She thought she was so clever. I wanted to tell my daughter he wasn't her real father and I wasn't her real mother. We found her at the bottom of a cave. No one else wanted her so we took her in and raised her. But that was too easy. She would never believe that. So instead, I told her again how full of shit she was.

Right up to your eyebrows, I said. It's like they popped open the top of your head and poured in buckets of the stuff. You stink of it to high heaven.

This time she didn't wince. She smiled at me. He told me to tell you that he was having a good time in heaven, she said. Without you.

As you can see, my daughter still makes up things. She still lies her head off all the time.

Which reminds me, I said to her, how's that piece of shit husband of yours?

Mom, you know we got divorced years ago. Why can't you keep up? Are you really so feeble-minded as all that?

The nurse on staff came into the room and gave me a bunch of pills. I wanted to fling them across the room. I actually did that once. The first month I was here. But oh boy, never again. I got such a talking to, for such a long time, that I wanted to die. Would have stabbed myself with a knife if one had been available.

So this time I put the pills into my mouth and swallowed them down. The nurse patted my shoulder and left the room to pour pills into some other inmate. Excuse me, *resident*.

That'll make you feel better, said my daughter.

Bullshit, I said. These pills make *them* feel better.

Where was I? she said in a dreamy kind of far away voice. Oh, yes. I remember. My dear old dead father. We had a good visit until he got on the subject of you. Then it was all downhill from there. He could not stop cussing you out. It was an amazing thing, Mom, truly amazing. He was so creative with his swearing. You inspire him. It's like you really made his life miserable and now he wants to be away from you. Forever. What exactly did you do to him?

If I ever did anything to him, which I most certainly did not, it was none of my daughter's business. I told her as much. Mind your own damn business, I said. We had a nice life together before you were born.

All the time I was growing up, she said, I expected him to walk in the door any minute. But that never happened.

I tried to change the subject. How are your bratty kids? I asked. Any of them sick? Any of them broke their arm or anything? Got trouble in school? Are they into drugs? I hope so. I hope they are royally fucked up.

I knew they were too old for school, but I was trying to get her to tell me how brain-dead I was for not remembering. She wouldn't have any of it. Stayed on me like a dog on a bone. You kept telling me he would come back, she said. Why did you do that? Did you enjoy making me feel terrible?

Memory is a funny thing. I *never* told her he was coming back. Not once. But she thinks I did.

Look, my darling daughter, I said. I was with him when he died. I'm the one who should be feeling terrible. I saw the blood and heard the last choking gasps.

Blah blah blah, said my daughter. Ancient history, Mother dear. Are we really going to roast that stale old chestnut again? Aren't you sick of it, Mom? Aren't you sick of the past?

Look who's talking, I said. You're riding my ass about what I did a billion and half fucking years ago. He fell on

MINIATURES   125

some goddamn rocks. It was an accident.

Well. We had pretty much reached our equilibrium point. She made me feel like crap and I returned the favor. We were both in a place that neither one of us would go to on our own. Together, though, we were amazing.

We *worked* at it. Our ritual.

Nothing to be ashamed of.

I do like the silence that descends on a room when the people in it stop talking. It feels like echoes are still there, floating around, making everything vibrate. Hum. That's a good feeling. I savored it for a while. We looked at each other, my daughter and me.

He really did come to me, she finally said in a whisper. In a dream. I dream about him, you know.

I knew.

He's there, she said. I don't even really remember what he looked like, but he's still alive in my head. He said he misses you.

Now that was dirty pool. She shouldn't be saying anything like that.

Bullshit, I said, but my voice broke. I *hate* that.

She didn't smile or acknowledge my weakness in any way. I appreciated that.

It's not, she said. It's not BS.

See? She can't even say the words. Has to use initials.

He was such a handsome man, I said to my daughter.

You climbed mountains with him, she said.

We made you, too, I said. The biggest goddamn mistake of my life.

I know, said my daughter. I know.

She said she had to be going. Some big conference of rock hounds somewhere. She was going to be gone for a few days. She would come back when it was over.

Haven't all you geologists found all the rocks yet? I said. What more is there for you to dig up?

You'd be surprised, she said.

I sighed. There's something for you in the closet, I told her.

She opened the closet door and found the dress I had made for her over the last couple of weeks.

Mom, she said, it's beautiful. She took it out and held it in front of her.

It didn't look half bad.

I'm glad you like it, I said.

I'm glad I gave you that sewing machine, she said. She kissed me on the forehead.

I grabbed her hand and held it tightly. She didn't try to pull away. I let go after a long time.

And then she was gone. She'd come back. She always did.

I liked her lie this time. That bit about finding her father in the clouds. That was a good one. Nice touch.

But it gave me a problem. It opened up my world. A split, right down the center of my room, with me straddling the gap. I was afraid I would fall into the rift.

Only one fix for that. I pulled the ragged edges together with my hands as best I could. I gave myself a bit of a head-ache, working the material. It was so tough. I held the edges

MINIATURES

against each other, then I maneuvered them to the sewing machine. I ran the edges through the machine so they were stitched together good and tight.

After I did that I felt a lot more comfortable. I didn't feel like pieces of my life were all over the place.

It made me remember when my husband used to sit with me just after my daughter got born. It was just the three of us then. Him holding my hand, me cradling my daughter and whispering to her how much I loved her and how neither of us would ever leave her.

Lies like that, the really good ones, are the best.

NATURALISTS

The twins stop to examine each crack in the sidewalk. What are you two looking for? asks Terrastina. We want to see how the pikas are doing, they say. I've never heard of pikas in the sidewalk, says Terrastina. Well, Mom, say the twins, let us explain something to you. Pikas who live in the woods get eaten by bigfoots. So some of them move into town where the bigfoots can't find them. I had no idea you knew so much about pika survival strategies, says Terrastina. The twins shrug. We know quite a bit about getting eaten up.

THE FATAL COLON

Mark suffered from debilitating diarrhea and entered an alternate universe seeking relief but accidently found himself in a world without punctuation where he was forced to speak and think without pauses or inflections and managed admirably until he wearied and faltered and inadvertently returned to his own universe like this:

DEADLINE

Of course I'll answer your questions. But you may be disappointed in my responses.

That's an easy one. Yes, I am the sum total of creation. What you would call the universe.

It seemed like time for people to have access to me.

Because the mystery of me has been troubling so many of you for so long. It's hampered your progress. I wanted to help you get past all the difficulty.

No, no. Not god. That's an outmoded concept. I don't like to be labeled with that term. So, no, I am not god.

The difference, for me, is that a god tells you how to behave in a moral sense. I don't have that perspective. I really don't know what's moral or immoral. I mean, beyond the obvious deeds everyone thinks you shouldn't do, like stealing and murdering and stuff like that.

But my point is that you don't need a god to tell you what's bad. Most of you already know what's bad.

No, I'm saying you're born with the knowledge.

Well, I see what you're getting at, and I suppose you're right, there are probably circumstances in which it's acceptable to do bad things for the greater good.

Yeah, or to defend one's self.

Okay, okay, we don't have to make a comprehensive list

MINIATURES   131

of all the exceptions.

Sorry. It's just that we don't want to spend all our time going over minutia, do we? Don't you have other things to ask me?

Blue.

Because it's the color of the best planets.

Yeah, red is pretty good too. Red would probably be my second favorite.

Wow. No one's ever asked me that one. Let's see, I was born way way back, so long ago I can't remember any of it. You all call it the big bang. That's as good a name as any, I suppose. But then, I've always thought beginnings are over-rated. I mean, the beginning of something is an instant in time. What's more important is what you do during all the subsequent instants.

Thank you. I don't have a lot of wisdom to give to people, but I do like that sentiment.

Um, yeah, I guess it would be good on a Christmas card.

Or a birthday card, sure.

No, I don't observe my birthday with a party or anything. Like I said, births are given more importance than they deserve.

My hair? Seriously? You want to know about my hair?

Well, okay. I did get it colored. Used to be golden, but I got tired of that. Too flashy. Now it's a deep reddish brown. I'm very happy with it.

Favorite movies? Really? That's your question? I'll have to think about it. To tell you the truth, I don't see too many. Can I get back to you on that?

No, not frivolous, exactly, but you have this opportunity that's pretty rare and maybe you might want to ask me about weightier matters.

Um, okay, yeah, like death.

Specific deaths? What do you mean?

Oh, your pet fish.

When was that?

When you were seven? And how did it die?

Too much food. Oh, dear.

So you're asking why I *let* you feed the fish too much when I knew that if it got too much food it would die.

I see.

Oh, right, right. That was the best pet you ever had.

Yes, I can understand how much you loved that fish.

Well, I don't know how to tell you this exactly, but I'm afraid I don't remember your pet fish.

Yeah, you mentioned how traumatic it was for you.

Sure, I can understand you want some answers. Everyone wants to make their pain go away.

No, I'm trying to remember, but even if I did remember I'm not sure I could offer you any real comfort. I don't have a lot of control over these things. Deaths happen.

I'm not being flip. Only stating a fact.

That's not true. I'm going to die like everyone else.

Why don't you believe me?

Well, there's this thing called the heat death of the universe. That's what *I* have to look forward to.

Yeah, maybe it would be better to go on to another topic.

Muffin? Your dog's name was Muffin?

MINIATURES

Oh, nothing wrong at all. I just never heard of a dog named Muffin. That's more of a cat's name isn't it?

I don't know, it seems like a cat name to me, not a dog name.

Well, yeah, it was your dog so you could name it anything you want.

I know. I wasn't trying to dispute that.

Oh dear. A car, you say? That's awful.

No, I didn't deliberately send that car to squash your dog on the road.

How do I know? Because I know.

Sure, I forgot about the fish, but I would have absolutely no reason whatsoever for killing your dog. None.

No, I don't have Alzheimer's. What kind of a question is that?

Listen, in the first place, universes don't get neurological diseases. And in the second place, anyone can forget things.

I know that, but it wasn't a big life event to *me*.

I'm not trying to be cruel. I'm only telling you the facts. What's important to you may not be important to someone else. That's all.

Okay, sure, people change so universes can change too. I'm not arguing that point. I'm only saying that I did not once have a personality disorder such that I tried to constantly kill people's pets.

No, I didn't know that you stopped keeping animals.

Everyone has trauma in their lives. Everyone loses things they love. You need to be strong and move on.

Well, that's not my fault.

I don't know. Probably nobody's. I told you: things happen. I could not possibly keep track of everything that has happened in my life. Nobody can.

It would be like you keeping track of every blood cell going through your heart. You can't do it.

I think you're mixing me up with god again. I am not omniscient or anything like that.

Well, okay, except god doesn't exist.

I do know.

Look, even if god did exist, he or she could not possibly keep track either.

Except I told you I don't have special powers like that. I'm nothing more than the universe. Pretty basic, you know. A few elements and a couple of universal laws. That's it.

Um, no. I don't think Muffin's in heaven.

Because I don't believe in heaven. I am the sum total, remember? Or is the concept too much for you to handle?

Sorry. I didn't mean to be so harsh.

Sorry, sorry. What's with the crying, now?

I said I was sorry.

It's all these questions about death, they're kind of getting to me. How old are you?

Seventeen? Huh.

Really?

Nothing, nothing.

I wasn't trying to say there's anything wrong with being seventeen. I was seventeen myself at one time. I'm only suggesting that maybe you don't quite have the maturity required to interview me.

MINIATURES   135

I'm not saying I'm all high and mighty, I'm saying I've been around a while and you haven't.

I suppose a novice's point of view can be valuable at times.

Yeah, I guess it shows initiative that you went after this interview.

Really? No one else wanted the job?

Well, I guess I should thank you for the favor, then.

But how did *you* get the assignment?

Oh, a contest. Like a lottery kind of thing?

Oh, sorry. You had to submit samples of your work to a panel of judges? How many applicants were there?

Four?

I'm sure they were *very* strong contenders.

Well, that *is* impressive.

Yeah, I have to say it's going pretty well.

No, I don't really have any suggestions for improvement.

Before we get to that, can you tell me why so few people wanted to interview me?

I don't often make myself available like this. I'd have thought there'd be lots of eager reporters out there wanting to get my story.

I see.

Oh. Cranky, huh?

And what else?

Phlegmatic? That's a bad thing?

I guess I can see that, but you're getting some usable answers out of me, aren't you?

You don't think it's a waste of time, do you?

Good. Because if you aren't getting what you want, it would be fine with me if you were to drop the whole idea. I've got lots of other things I could be doing.

That's not what I meant. I think you're great.

No, I am *not* just saying that. You ask a lot of unexpected questions.

No, I'm saying that's *good*.

What?

I don't know that.

Seriously.

I am *not* kidding. There's no way I could possibly know when you are going to die. And if I did, I'm sure I wouldn't tell you.

Because *that* would be cruel.

No, I don't know.

No.

Look, I told you already. I have no special powers. I'm not god or god-like in any way.

I said *no*.

Oh, jeez, you are so sensitive. You sure you want to be a reporter?

It's not a crack. It's a question.

The kind of question you ask a reporter when they're getting all hysterical with their interviewee and crying.

There, there.

You'll feel better soon. Good to get all that pent up frustration out. Tears are very cleansing, you know.

No, I didn't invent tears. They were an accident. Most of everything happened by accident.

MINIATURES   137

Sure, I can understand that.

I'll wait for you to collect yourself.

You've asked me that already, I think. The answer is that I don't know.

Nope, the future is a mystery. Death is a mystery.

The thing is, no other animal much cares about that stuff. It's only humans.

That wouldn't be so bad. You go about your life and one day—poof!—you're gone. Painless and quick.

That's the second time you've called me cruel.

I'm not hurt, I'm only saying you might want to watch that if you intend to continue in this profession.

What?

You mean if I wasn't the universe?

Well, I never thought of that. I suppose I would consider being a star.

Because they have a lot of power. They essentially make everything else because they produce all the heavy elements.

What?

Your nose?

No, I don't have that ability.

Your nose is perfectly fine. You don't need to "fix" it.

I am completely serious.

I don't know why you don't believe me.

What's that, now?

What? Your sister died?

Oh.

Oh, my.

That's terrible.

I didn't know.

Well, again, please understand that I am *not* trying to be cruel, but if you think about it, it's not much different from your fish or your dog. People die too, just like pets.

Oh, I wish I could bring people back, but I can't.

Yeah, I tried.

Just to see if I could.

Not recently, but believe me, it wouldn't be different now.

I'm pretty sure ghosts are figments of your imagination.

That's right, a kind of wish fulfillment.

You could be right.

I'm very aware that I don't know everything.

No kidding? What's she doing when you see her?

That must bring you some comfort.

Not even a little?

I'm sorry to hear that.

Now that you mention it, some physicists have been saying I'm some kind of ghost or hologram or something. Physicists really get on my nerves sometimes. So sure of themselves.

Oh, right, we were talking about your sister.

I'm really very sorry.

Yeah, that is way too young to die.

Sure, I can see why you asked me those questions, but I wasn't holding anything back. I'm not holding anything back now.

Well, did you try talking to your family? Sometimes they can be a help.

Oh.

I see.

So they don't want to talk about her at all?

That's sad.

Do you have friends who remember her?

Well, then, you should talk to them. It'll be good for you.

It'll get better, believe me. Pain fades, you know.

No, I didn't plan it that way. It's simply the way it came out in the mix.

Yeah, I'll keep an eye out for her, but I have to tell you, don't expect anything.

Promise.

Really, I promise. If I see her, you'll be the first to know.

Sure, I'll give you a hug.

There. How does that feel?

Yeah, I guess it's time. It's been a long interview.

Oh, don't worry about it.

I'm sure you'll do fine. Your editor will be very happy.

No, I don't need to see the article beforehand. I trust you to do a good job.

You're welcome.

Okay, one last question. Shoot.

Well, I love everything.

Oh, you mean have I ever *been* in love? I have to tell you, that's a human question.

But, you see, there is only one of me. I couldn't fall in love with another.

I would say I'm *alone* a lot, but I'm not ever *lonely*.

Sure.

Thanks.

Great to meet you too.

Oh, I'm sure we will. I think it's going to be hard not to. You're going to really be something. People are going to hear from you in the future.

Yeah.

Bye.

Love you too.

THE CONSEQUENCES
OF NOT AVERTING YOUR EYES

Cornstalk Waterfall owned only a cup, for drinking water, and a cloak, for modesty. One day he saw a man drinking water from his cupped hands. Cornstalk realized his own cup was superfluous so he gave it away. Then he saw another man walking the streets naked. Cornstalk considered the beauty of the man and his way of living and donated his cloak to charity. He then encountered a man without arms. Cornstalk discarded his own arms. People stared at Cornstalk. Cornstalk looked back. Seeing nothing in their eyes, Cornstalk offered passersby his own soul. None accepted, none felt deprived.

THE HIDDEN LIVES OF PUPPETS

His face was my first image, right after he sewed the buttons on the end of my sock body. The green thread, I think, must have given my buttons vision, like a retina. Light filled me and I saw him squinting to make sure the needle went through the button hole, my eye hole.

That was years ago. He used to put on shows for children's birthday parties. I was a dinosaur. It was a good thing to be—kids never get tired of dinosaurs. I got lots of stage time. He really liked me.

I gave hundreds of performances. We had this routine where I was a baby dinosaur who couldn't find her mother. I searched and searched, with him sliding me across the stage. I found exotic creatures, one by one, on his other hand, and I asked all of them where my mother was.

No one knew where she was. I felt sad. He wouldn't let me cry, though. I kept searching until the audience saw my mother upstage and screamed and hollered at me until I turned around and saw her. I was so happy to find her. Far from deserting me, she had been out getting food for me to eat. She scolded me for leaving the dinosaur nest. Then she hugged me, and we both went back to the nest.

Such a sweet story. The kids loved it. It taught them to be obedient to their parents and that they could be independent.

MINIATURES

All at the same time. I never tired of performing that story, but he did, after a couple of decades. Truth is, he got tired of puppets in general. He moved on to magic shows.

I'm all dusty and threadbare, now. My eye buttons have loosened. I can hardly see through one of them because the button is flopped over and the other one is crooked so what I do see is not only blurred but tilted. It is dark anyway, so I wouldn't see much even if I had perfect vision. I have existed in this state for a long time.

Should I complain? No use, I suppose. I sometimes feel like crying, but I can't do that without him. I can't do any kind of movement without him.

I hear voices. Not his. Light floods my buttons. I am filled with energy.

"Have we checked in this closet yet?"

"Man, Uncle Norm had a lot of junk, didn't he?"

"He made most of this stuff for his act."

"Too bad he didn't get rid of it before he died. Now we have to take care of it."

Died? He died? Have I been in the closet that long? I am disoriented and unsure of how to respond. He could always make me smile or laugh or look sad. Him. It was all him. Oh, we worked together, but he was the engine that made us go. Now I don't know what to do.

"Hey, look, here are all his puppets."

"I always wished he hadn't stopped doing those puppet shows. I loved them when I was a kid."

"Let's haul the box out and have a look."

I am jostled and bumped. I fall against my mother. Green

MARIO MILOSEVIC

felt skin. Red buttons for eyes. She looks at me blankly. I want only to cry. Again. Please let me cry. I want to feel puppet tears.

"Wow, I remember all of these. There's the armadillo and the kangaroo. Here's the bear and the ant. That was a great story. The ant takes on the bear—and wins. Oh, and hey, how about that, the dinosaur who lost its mother."

"You remember all of these?"

"Sure. The dinosaur story made me cry. But then it was all okay because she finds her mother. See?"

"If you say so. Should I leave you with your memories for a while? I could go get the last of the kitchen stuff out of here."

"Just sit with me for a while, won't you? I want to remember Uncle Norm."

"You always said he was a cold bastard."

"I did *not.*"

"Sure you did. I remember."

"Well, if I did, it doesn't matter now. He had problems relating to people, but he was wonderful when he put on these shows."

Being a puppet is not the most liberating thing in the world. We are so dependent on another person. Now that my person is gone, I begin to see that my empty life is going to continue forever. An endless expanse of nothing: no activity, no stimulation.

But wait.

What's this?

A hand fills me. Oh my! Memories come rushing back:

me walking upright, me floating above the stage, me filled up with power and purpose.

"Looks like that puppet fits you perfectly."

"Yes, isn't that funny. I've never put it on my hand before."

"Maybe you want to revive the act?"

"No, that would be silly. I'm no performer."

"You don't have to be. Didn't Uncle Norm always tell you the puppets had a life of their own? They did the acting, he just went along for the ride."

"Oh, that was just him talking. Of course the puppets were nothing without him. That was actually the one thing that made him special."

This new hand, it is smaller than his was, but that does not matter. It shakes itself, as though trying to throw off dust. I rattle and shiver. Much of my dust falls away. With her other hand, this new person smooths down my head and my body, pushing even more dust off of me. It falls in clumps and gathers on the floor.

She looks into my eyes.

With her hand as still as a rock, I tremble. I tremble on my own, with no assistance from her or anyone.

"What do you see there?"

"These buttons. They look familiar."

"Familiar? They must be forty years old. Maybe more."

"That would be about right. I think they're from a dress I had when I was five. I outgrew it and gave the buttons to Uncle Norm. He was always looking for buttons for his puppets. He would go through dozens of them before he found the right one for a particular puppet."

"Huh. That's amazing if you really remember it."

"I remember it. Why wouldn't I? I always thought he seemed like a sad person. Even when I was a kid I noticed it. I gave him the buttons to cheer him up. It was a very sweet moment because he *thanked* me."

"Okay. That makes sense. I wasn't trying to start anything."

Her buttons? I'm seeing through her buttons? I want to communicate with her. I want to tell her how much her gift has meant to me.

"I'm sorry. I didn't mean to snap at you. Here, this will cheer you up."

"Oh, yes. Put on the mother dinosaur."

"That's what I'm doing. Is this how you hold it?"

"Kind of. Move your arm over to the side a little. Now try to hook your hand so it curves like a jaw."

"Like this?"

"Not bad. Now say something in dinosaur."

"I'm huuuuuunnnnnngreeeeeeeeeee."

I hear my mother's voice. I tremble. I turn to her. My puppeteer's hand turns. My button eyes meet my mother's button eyes. I feel her love for me. It has been so long since I have seen her at all. I leap towards her.

"Ouch!"

"What? What is it?"

"This puppet, it moved."

"What do you mean it moved?"

"It moved. It moved. It scratched me. Look."

MINIATURES

She flings me to the floor. Oh no. Oh no. I should have been more careful. My insides are rough and scratchy. I hurt her.

What do I do now? My button eyes look up to the ceiling. I see nothing there for me.

Please pick me up again.

Please give me life.

"Damn, that's quite a scratch. Let me put something on it."

"Ouch ouch ouch. There must be a needle in it or something. How can it hurt so much?"

"Maybe that's why Uncle Norm gave up the business. Maybe his puppets were attacking him."

"That's crazy."

"Yeah. I know."

"But just to be safe. Let's throw out the whole bunch of them."

Throw out?

I groan. Or try to. I also attempt to cry. Again. I concentrate my will and push against the floor with all my strength. I feel a very slight trembling. Maybe more a wish for movement than actual movement itself.

My button eyes hang by only a thread.

"Hey, will you look at that?"

"What is it?"

"The dinosaur puppet. It's got something leaking from its eyes."

"Let me see."

She lifts me from the floor. I feel fingers wrap around my

buttons. My eyes.

The pressure grows, straining the thread.

Then a snap.

And another.

"That was easy."

"Yeah, they came right off."

"What was it leaking?"

"If I didn't know any better, I'd say they were tears."

I am plunged into darkness again.

I have no eyes.

"Funny, isn't it? Uncle Norm never wanted any of his puppets to cry. I remember he told me. Said it was sentimental and he wanted to avoid that."

"Probably afraid the kids watching the show would take it too seriously if he had puppets crying."

"Probably. But you know, it bothered me when I was a kid. It was like he didn't want people to express emotion."

"So he *was* a cold-hearted bastard."

"We shouldn't talk about him like that, now that he's dead."

"Yeah, I guess you're right."

"I think I'll keep the buttons, though. Just for a reminder."

"Well, they're yours, after all. From your dress when you were a kid."

"What should we do with the puppet?

"Pretty useless without the eyes."

"No one will want it. Let's just toss it in the garbage."

"I am so ready to be out of here."

MINIATURES

"Me too. Suddenly, just being in his house feels kind of creepy."

I want my hearing gone, too. Like my vision. I prefer the mercy of silence with my darkness.

So much more comforting that way.

I yearn for emptiness.

AN UNNATURAL HISTORY
OF SCARECROWS

Straw for guts, as a rule. Also for limbs and general bulk. Other materials will do, but straw is always available so why not use it? For clothes, torn and raggedy castoffs, often patched, often faded. It gives the scarecrow a tough look, like they don't care about getting down and dirty when the occasion warrants such actions. They'll wade into a fight if they have to.

Sticks will do for hands and feet, although neither is truly necessary. Crows have vivid imaginations and they can extrapolate from straw limbs to fingers and toes with little effort.

The head should be sculpted from burlap, again stuffed with straw. The eyes, nose, and mouth painted on. You can make it menacing if you want, but it isn't necessary. Just the suggestion of a human face is supposed to be enough to frighten the crows.

A hat will complete the look. You should have a hat, unless you elect to give your scarecrow a head of hair, but such affectations generally detract from the overall effect. You can make a hat look much more natural than fake hair.

The alert student will note that the scarecrow, as outlined above, does not do what it purports to do. In other words, crows are generally not frightened by scarecrows.

This is no one's fault. All inventions go through stages. At one time, in the distant past, I believe that such avatars did scare crows, but over the years the crows grew accustomed to them and learned that they did no harm whatsoever. We must now apply our intellect and imaginations and concoct the next stage in the evolution of scarecrows. Any suggestions as to how we might go about this?

Ah, yes, you with your hand up.

Pardon me?

You're saying we should interview a crow.

Now class, calm down and save your snickering. It is not such a bad idea. In fact, I think it might be an excellent idea. Let's begin by interviewing a crow.

Yes, here's one flying by now. Excuse me. Crow. May I trouble you for a few moments?

Excellent, yes, thank you for stopping.

No, this won't take long.

What's that?

You say you're apolitical? I understand completely. But you see, this has nothing to do with politics.

No, I'm not asking you to sign any kind of petition or recall effort. I am interested in ascertaining what you are afraid of.

Yes, of course, I understand your suspicions, but I assure you my motives are benign. I wish to produce a kind of scare device which will keep you and your kind from our agricultural regions.

I understand you need to eat, but we wish that you would eat elsewhere.

Of course you can refuse to answer. It is a free country, but I would be remiss if I did not inform you of the fact that if we do not produce a suitable device, we will be forced to take more drastic measures, up to and including the killing of crows.

Oh, dear. Are you all right?

I didn't mean to upset you.

No, it is not that I *want* to kill crows, it is that I may be *forced* to do so, for our own survival. I'm sure you understand.

Oh. You don't understand. Well, that's understandable.

So you will not answer my questions?

Very well.

I wish you the best. Thank you for your time.

And there goes the crow, flying in a decidedly crooked line. That did not go so well at all. Are there any other suggestions?

Yes, the young lady in the back. You wish to offer an idea?

Ahem, well, yes I see where you are going with that. If we were in fact to *become* crows we would, by necessity, be aware of what we feared. But how, may I ask, do you propose to turn any of us into crows?

I thought so.

Any other suggestions?

A show of hands, please. Surely *someone* has some ideas. You are the most advanced class in the academy. Am I to deduce from the general lack of hands showing that my most gifted students are unable to offer a single viable path to success in the present situation? Or are you afraid to look foolish? What have I said about such fears?

Yes, the young man in the front row.

Exactly. There are no foolish ideas, only fools who will not attempt to create ideas.

So let me ask you, one more time, how might we go about creating the next generation of scarecrow?

Nothing?

No one will even attempt a proposal?

Class, what is all that ruckus?

Calm down, please.

What are you pointing at?

Ah, I see. A flock of crows. Yes, and they appear to be heading in this direction. Well, this is fortuitous. Perhaps the pressure of an actual attack will spur you to heights of accomplishment.

Why should we take cover? You do not fear the crows do you? If anyone should, it is me.

Now class, those crows appear to be upset and they wish to unleash their fury on us. Here is your moment. Seize it! How will you scare them away? By what mechanism or sorcery?

No. No. It will not do to run away. Not now. Come back! Class, obey me! Return to your seats this instant.

Yes, my clothes are torn, I see that. My limbs are thin and bent. But why do you point at me so? My head is smooth and bald. What did you expect?

Where are you going?

Come back.

They do not fear me. They will be on me in an instant.

Class.

Come back.

Class, please return. Don't leave me alone. I cannot face them any longer.

THE CLEX ARE OUR FRIENDS

INTRODUCTION

You are on the winning side of a prolonged and bloody interplanetary conflict.

Congratulations!

You can thank your planet and its glorious principles, your commanding officers, your buddies in arms, and yourself.

Now for the next phase.

You have been ordered into Cleck, the battlefield planet, to help restore order and civil society. You will encounter alien races and alien customs.

Many of these will be confusing. What's worse, many of them will be dangerous. This booklet will attempt to help you with both situations, as well as prepare you for your mission.

This booklet is encrypted so only you can read it. Do not fear a security breach if it should fall into alien hands, however, do exercise prudent caution and discretion in its use.

It is to your advantage to study the contents of this booklet very carefully. Your life may depend on it.

Also, remember at all times that you are a representative of Earth. Please uphold the highest standards of morality and conduct.

SOME HISTORY

You are on Cleck to do a vital job, namely: secure the planet.

Of course, this simple statement does not convey the full flavor of your duties.

Allow me, in this short space and in my own way, to explain more fully the parameters of your mission.

Your duty on Cleck is to remove any Stewn left behind after the final battle of the war.

As you may or may not know, Stewn are descended from Clex. Centuries ago the Clex developed space travel. Some of the Clex left their planet to colonize another. Those migrant Clex evolved into Stewn.

A few years ago, the Stewn returned to the planet Cleck to claim what they thought was rightfully theirs. This included massive mineral deposits, which the Clex have since graciously offered to us in exchange for cleaning up the Stewn. This is indeed a fortunate circumstance for which we as a planet can be grateful. All we have to do is come in and mine it out. After the Stewn are gone.

It goes without saying that the Stewn invasion of Cleck was completely contrary to accepted norms of interstellar law. Earth stepped in to stop the invasion and right a terrible wrong. Our motive was the restoration of justice.

We lost a lot of good people in the process. Some may have been your comrades.

But it was worth it. The Clex needed us. They really did.

So here we are. Revel in your duties. Accept the accolades that are sure to be showered upon you.

MINIATURES

EQUIPMENT

TRANSLATOR. You have been issued a translation device. Keep it on your person at all times. The Clex are a touchy species. If they believe you do not understand them, they are liable to grab you with some vehemence and may inadvertently tear off one of your limbs. This will upset them terribly. Also, make sure your translation device has fresh batteries.

GOGGLES. Air on Cleck is very moist and has a high acidic content. This does not bother the Clex, but will make your eyes burn if you are exposed to it too long. The specially designed goggles you have been issued will alleviate this problem.

MRE. You can't eat Clex food. If you tried, it would eat you. Bring your own food.

The above items are in addition to your standard gear, NOT a replacement for same.

FIRST CONTACT

Clex have very long tongues. Two of them each. Upon first meeting you, they will extend one or more of their tongues, place them on your person, and taste you for several seconds. Do not be alarmed. Few of your fellow soldiers have succumbed to the corrosive juices that coats a Clex tongue. And the ones that did weren't wearing proper gear no matter what rumors you've heard.

After the tasting, be sure to spit on the ground. This is their custom, and by doing so you convey the message that you respect their customs.

Your spitting will elicit strange buzzing noises from the

Clex. Our intelligence has convinced us that this is their equivalent of laughter. It is an indication that they appreciate the expulsion of saliva. Use this fact to help you. Those soldiers who do not spit sometimes end up in sick bay with severe injuries.

CLEX CHARACTER

We know you've heard stories about the Clex. That they are cowardly, that they eat children, and that they will not defend themselves. Don't you believe it. It has been widely reported that no Clex has ever been seen eating its own child. Not once.

Also, while it is true that they cowered in their cities while their enemies, the Stewn, rained destruction across their planet, when it came time, the Clex were very willing to help us defeat the Stewn. They offered us unlimited access to their food stores, even though we could not eat any of it, and they tended to some of our wounded when we could not get to them. A few of those even survived.

You may also hear rumors that the Clex resent our presence. Nothing could be further from the truth. They respect our fighting ability and our amazing spirit and skills.

The cold hard truth is this: Clex can fight but usually choose not to because of their religious beliefs, which include a strong pacifist streak.

Recall our devotion to religious freedom. It is a cornerstone of a humanitarian society. Do not mock or criticize the Clex for adhering to their religious principles, even if it puts you in danger. You're a soldier. You live for danger, right?

MINIATURES

Remember, we are here to help the Clex, not to judge them.

FAMILY LIFE

After initial contact with a Clex, you may be invited into their homes. Accept the invitation gracefully.

The Clex couple constantly. Several times a day. Your presence in their house will not deter them. Try not to comment. Also, try not to watch. For your own good.

Once in a Clex home, you will be pounced on by their children. Do not be alarmed. Few of them are lethal. Slimy and smelly, but not lethal.

Clex generally have many children. Each house will harbor at least a dozen, often more. This does not mean they breed uncontrollably. On the contrary, they could in fact have dozens more children than they do, but they restrain themselves to help preserve the resources of their planet. Such an attitude is well worthy of our respect.

You will sometimes be offered one or more of their children as a gift. If this happens, you must immediately hit the button on your translator marked with the big NO in bright red glowing letters. The phrase that comes out of it will be the Clex version of the following:

"I greatly appreciate your kind offer but must decline at this time. I hope you understand."

Practice hitting this button rapidly and accurately.

The Clex like to sing. At first their songs will be hard on your ears. Think of pigs going to slaughter. Mixed with fingernails on chalkboard. Sound disgusting? Well, music is an acquired taste. You'll get used to it.

FIELD WORK

Although it is fun and instructive, not to mention horizon broadening, to spend time with aliens and alien culture, do not forget your reason for being on Cleck. Be as polite as necessary to the Clex, but keep your wits about you and focus on the mission.

Which is killing Stewn.

The best way to kill a Stewn is by blunt force. You have been issued a metal baton for the purpose. If you should lose it, a heavy stick will do. You can find an abundant assortment of good strong sticks in the Cleck countryside. They will have thorns on them. Wear your gloves.

Stewn used to congregate in great flocks, gathering in more or less exposed locations to launch their attacks on Clex houses and towns. That was before we defeated them. Now they generally cower in caves and such.

This one fact solves the issue of telling a Clex from a Stewn. Clex are our friends and greet us openly. Stewn hide. Burn this fact into your brain, because, honestly, there's no other way to tell them apart. They look almost identical.

I don't need to tell you that looks can be deceiving. Clex are our friends. Stewn are our enemies. Very simple.

By the time you see them, the Stewn will be mostly unarmed. Many will be feeble from lack of food. After all, we cut off their supply lines.

A good number of the Stewn will be close to death when you find them anyway, so you may think of your actions as being merciful. Humanitarian would be a good word to keep in mind. Especially when you return to Earth after your mission and are asked about your activities by civilians.

Remember not to disturb the Clex while you go about your duties. They do not like to be bothered with such things. The Clex, as you may have surmised from what you have read so far, are a very refined and honorable species. They are expected to be a great help to us when we gather our forces to invade the Stewn home planet.

With luck, you will be part of that campaign, but do not get ahead of yourself. That is at least a year or so in the future.

SOME CAUTIONS

Occasionally a Clex will offer to accompany you on your missions. This is a tricky situation. In general it is best to discourage such participation; however, certain individual Clex can be persistent and persuasive.

Here is the problem: Once a Stewn gets within smelling distance of a Clex, all its latent hostility and murderous intent rises to the surface and you have a very dangerous Stewn on your hands.

The remedy is to keep Clex away from Stewn. If a Clex offers to help, use your NO button. If that does not work, allow the Clex to come with you, but dispatch it at your earliest opportunity.

Away from any prying eyes.

You will thank yourself later.

SOME FINAL THOUGHTS

Rumors are a part of military life. We understand this. We know you hear many distasteful stories about Clex society and Clex as a species.

Try to ignore these. They will only poison your attitude and make you reluctant to carry out your very important duties.

Remember that the Clex are our friends. As such, we do not betray or hurt them unless absolutely necessary for the good of the mission, which, ultimately, is for their good as well.

Use your superior intellect and killing power with discretion. Harm a Clex only when circumstances make all other options unfeasible.

THANK YOU

Finally, on behalf of a grateful planet, which will benefit tremendously from your brave and necessary mission, let me offer my heartfelt thanks for your unselfish and unflinching duty.

You make us all proud to be human.

GENEALOGY

One of my ancestors was the kind of insect that eats anything even its own children.

One of my ancestors gave birth to a sterile baby who therefore never extended his branch of the family tree.

One of my ancestors lived in the sea and was constantly wary of attacks from other ocean creatures.

One of my ancestors started a family of five children and then left them all one day and spent the rest of her years atop a cold and barren mountain.

One of my ancestors remembered a time when the Earth had no multi-celled creatures.

One of my ancestors looked just like the oak tree rooted at the corner a block away from my house.

One of my ancestors was a cheetah who had to kill an antelope every week just to survive another seven days.

One of my ancestors was a snake who crawled on the ground

and ate her meals whole.

One of my ancestors had wings made of feathers but dreamed of building houses out of stone.

One of my ancestors was killed when lava from a volcano turned him into a fossil that a geologist found ten million years later and discarded as being too ordinary.

One of my ancestors killed many people and was finally killed himself when he fell from a mountain path to a field of rocks a thousand feet below.

One of my ancestors discovered religion and used it to make other people feel as though they could not live in this world.

One of my ancestors flew to the moon before anyone knew what the moon was but did not tell anyone because she thought the moon was better off without anymore visitors.

One of my ancestors could foretell the future but chose not to do so as the knowledge only made him so terrified of life he would remain in bed for weeks at a time.

One of my ancestors lived her last few years as a tattoo on a biker's upper arm right next to the heart with the sword through it.

One of my ancestors was so small he lived in the arteries of a

MINIATURES

hummingbird.

One of my ancestors was harpooned by a whaling ship but lived to tell the story many times.

One of my ancestors was crushed by a falling meteorite.

One of my ancestors did not speak for sixty years then said good bye and died an hour later.

One of my ancestors ate only a certain kind of leaf that she found by following the flight paths of birds who nested only in those kinds of trees.

One of my ancestors was a peach who lived in the middle part of an old limb on a worn peach tree.

One of my ancestors spoke to rocks who spoke back to her.

One of my ancestors emerged from the sun and spent a million years wandering the solar system until she decided to settle down here on Earth.

One of my ancestors was a crab who could never get enough of the salt spray splashing his shell.

One of my ancestors sulked whenever it looked as though he was about to be served a helping of broccoli.

One of my ancestors was a centaur who loved women and horses but would never allow any of them to love him.

One of my ancestors was allergic to bee stings and never ate honey.

One of my ancestors grew a rack of antlers every year and no one not even the other bucks ever said a word about it.

One of my ancestors swam the length of the Mississippi River upstream.

One of my ancestors was born in a garbage dump and spent all her days there and could not think of a better way to live.

One of my ancestors stole a horse and was hung by his angry fellow citizens.

One of my ancestors regularly drank six beers a day and smoked two packs of cigarettes but would not drive because it was too dangerous.

One of my ancestors took five years out of his life to count the grains of sand on the beach behind his house.

One of my ancestors was the voice for a famous cartoon character no one remembers anymore.

One of my ancestors built a ship to bring invaders from one

part of the world to destroy the people in another part of the world.

One of my ancestors was the first creature to lie to another creature.

One of my ancestors had a long tail that she liked to curl around the branches of trees from where she would drop fruit on creatures passing beneath her and laugh until her tail uncurled and she fell on her head and forgot who or what or where she was.

FEAR OF LUCILLE

Lucille was born surrounded by a rich and unearthly glow. When she was two years old, her parents discovered that anyone she touched for longer than a few minutes was cured of any ill health they may have had.

"We can't allow our daughter to go on doing this," said Lucille's father after a few days of thought. "If the rest of the world found out about Lucille's power, millions would want to use her and her life would become a nightmare. It is our duty to protect her from such a fate."

Lucille's mother thought that preventing her child from bringing goodness to the world would be nightmarish, too, but she let herself be persuaded by her husband.

For one year they did not allow Lucille to touch anyone and prevented anyone from touching her.

Lucille's glow grew steadily dimmer until it disappeared. She became sullen and began wetting her bed in her sleep.

When Lucille was three years, old her mother held her for an hour, but her mother's terrible bronchitis, which she had mysteriously contracted a few months before, would not go away.

"There," said Lucille's father upon seeing this. "Now she is safe. Now she is like us."

Lucille pushed against her mother and tried to escape

MINIATURES   169

from her strong arms.

"Yes," said her mother in a rasping, labored voice. "Now I feel much better." She held Lucille as though the girl was a struggling cat.

Lucille's father listened to his wife's wheezy, gasping words. He smiled and stroked his daughter's hair. "I feel better, too," he said.

HOUSING PROJECT

The twins tell Terrastina they have decided to live in the closet. Just bring our dinners in there from now on, they say. We'll leave the dishes outside the door when we are done. Okay, says Terrastina, have a good time in your closet. We will, say the twins. They spend no more than two minutes behind the closed door, then they come out. How do you like your closet? asks Terrastina. It was pretty dark, say the twins. We're going to go back when it's not *quite* so dark. Well, says Terrastina, I'll be sure to visit you.

LEAVES

My seven-year-old daughter Myra used to dance with the oak tree in our back yard. She would circle it in a complex pattern of loops and curls that sometimes took her a few yards from the tree but always brought her back to it.

I remember watching her one autumn through the basement window. From where I stood I saw the lawn, silvery with frost, stretched out like a carpet between me and the tree. The oak's leaves had turned a pale yellow. I watched Myra's shoes crush the frozen blades of grass as she ran around the tree. I envied Myra her carefree play with its innocence and blithe inventiveness: There was no room for dull old reality to spoil the game.

As I watched, an unaccustomed wave of melancholy washed over and through me. Seeing Myra with the oak, I felt myself infinitely distant from my own beginnings. I could not understand Myra's dance, nor the part the oak played in the choreography.

I watched until Myra grew tired of the game. She skipped off to another part of the yard and I was left alone with the tree.

I stared at it for a long time. The leaves seemed to tremble, but I was sure their barely perceptible motion was the work of my own eyeballs, not the still air. After some moments I saw one of the leaves detach itself from a branch and fall to the ground.

A falling leaf is an unremarkable event, and yet it struck me immediately that most people rarely see a leaf fall in quite the way I saw this one fall. There were no other leaves on the ground: this was the first. I sensed a chance to observe a process from beginning to end and moved quickly to the window. I pressed my nose against the pane and held my hands above my head on the glass. The leaf rested on blades of grass like a suspended canvas tent. I stared at it for a couple of seconds and held my breath to prevent fogging the glass. I tilted my eyes upward and fixed my stare on the leaves bunched atop the rough-surfaced trunk.

The first leaf must have been a signal. Soon many leaves began falling slowly. They shivered as they descended through the air to touch the lawn. Though at first they all seemed to fall at once, I soon determined that no pair detached themselves at exactly the same time. They followed a grand design where each patiently waited for its turn to join the others on the ground. A circle of leaves began to form around the base of the tree. It grew thicker as the branches became bare.

I discovered I had not been breathing for some time and my eyelids had frozen open. Alarmed, I tried to move my limbs, but they were held solidly in place. I could not move a bone or muscle. I could not even express my puzzlement and growing panic because my face was also immobile. My stuck eyeballs fixed my center of vision just below the leaves remaining on the tree. Tears began to well up in my eyes and drip onto the floor. I felt my toes lengthen and break through

MINIATURES

the concrete of the floor.

Outside, the trees seemed to stare back at me. I felt a fear like I imagined a claustrophobe must feel: trapped, powerless, smothered. At that moment the tree seemed unyielding and terrifying and I thought briefly that it served me right. I should not have been watching it so closely. I was not equipped to cope with the genesis of physical events. Not like Myra, who, like all children, copes with beginnings every day.

My tears began to run more freely. They dripped through the floor, touched my branching feet, and pulsed up through my legs and body to my arms, impossibly high over my head. My fingers swelled as liquid flooded into my hands.

Most of the leaves were gone from the tree. I estimated the first one had fallen not more than twenty minutes ago, and now there were only isolated clumps and solo leaves that clung like drops of moisture on a cold glass of water.

"Daddy!"

Myra called to me. She seemed far away, but the sound of her voice was something I could hold onto. I struggled against myself and loosened my hands until I could move them down to my legs. I pulled at my thigh violently until I released my foot. Concrete dust filled the air around my calves. I pulled out my other leg and turned to face my daughter.

"Daddy, what are you doing?"

I rubbed my eyes, and breathed heavily. "I was just looking at the leaves."

She ran to me and hugged my legs. I touched the top of her head and looked out at the tree again. It seemed different from before. I felt an ache in my chest and was acutely aware of the blood surging through my veins.

My daughter released me and stepped back. "Don't you ever do that again," she said. "You're lucky I was here."

I looked at the two holes in the floor where my feet had been and thought: Yes, this time I was lucky.

Next spring my daughter was six months older. The tree, mysteriously, did not survive the winter and I had to cut it down and chop it up for firewood. Each time I put a piece of it in the fireplace I felt as though I was cremating a bit of my own flesh.

Eventually I fed the whole tree to the flames and it turned to ash. I realized, reluctantly, that my flirtation with beginnings had had no permanent effect on me, either ill or benign, except that ever since that season with the tree, I have sometimes found myself scratching at the buds that have been sprouting on the tips of my fingers.

SOLACE

I woke up one night from a disturbing dream. The details of the dream drifted away, but the unsettled feeling persisted. I lived by the sea and the sound of the waves at that moment felt too loud to endure. I looked across my bedroom and saw my ghost sitting in the chair next to the window.

"Am I dead?" I asked.

"No," said my ghost. "I'm just tired of living inside you." He looked out the window. His expression reminded me of a child about to eat a piece of candy.

"Don't be ridiculous," I said. "You can't leave me until I die."

My ghost laughed, stood, opened the window, and stepped through it. I went to the window and looked outside. I saw no trace of my ghost. He was gone.

My belly felt empty. My head ached. Pain wrapped my joints and I shivered with cold. I fell back on my bed and stared at the ceiling. I hurt more than I had ever hurt before.

My life changed. I suddenly felt like I had no purpose at all. It was a strange feeling. Before that night, I was a conscientious and hard-working citizen of my community. I had a good job as a lawyer for the county, I did volunteer work at the local school, and I maintained an active social life. I went out with many charming and beautiful women.

But none of those activities interested me in the least anymore. I quit my job, shunned all social contact, and told the school exactly what I thought of their bratty little pupils. No one was interested in spending time with me anymore. Which suited me fine. I wanted to be alone.

Without an adequate income, I could no longer make payments on my house. The bank repossessed it and booted me onto the streets.

I took to the road, hitchhiking across the country and living under bridges with drifters and hoboes. I got to know other people whose ghosts had deserted them. We all had this vague feeling of being wrong in the world. We noted the feeling, remarked on its power over us, but found no way to connect with each other as human beings. I had a notion that we should work to form a community, all of us without our ghosts, but that never happened.

Finding food was always a problem. I learned to glean good stuff from dumpsters. That was depressing at first; then it became a challenge. I begged for food too, but the dumpsters were more efficient.

Somewhere in the third or fourth year after the departure of my ghost I found myself in a desert city trying to fit into the street culture there. It wasn't working. They were highly suspicious of me. I took the hint and began walking out of town. No particular destination in mind, just walking.

Soon I was in the desert. I saw a ghost. He was wandering through the desert, lost. He was not my ghost, but he triggered a feeling of compassion in me I had thought was permanently gone from my life.

MINIATURES

I approached him and asked if he needed help.

The ghost did not want to talk to me at first. He turned and walked away. I thought about letting him go. After all, live and let live had become my motto. But I wanted to know more about his circumstances. I followed him. He tried to brush me off. I persisted.

"Is your host dead?" I asked.

"No," replied the ghost. "He just didn't want me anymore. Said I was too much of a burden."

It had not occurred to me that people could get rid of their own ghosts.

"I could be your host," I said.

"Thanks," said the ghost, "but I don't think we would be a good fit."

"How do you know?"

"If you have to ask . . ." said the ghost. He accelerated his pace and was soon out of my reach, then out of my sight.

I put my hand against a saguaro cactus and breathed heavily. I cursed myself for hoping and kept walking.

I began seeing other ghosts. Once I noticed a few of them, it seemed they were everywhere. But none of them wanted to talk to me.

I ended up back in a village by the sea. I lived on the beach. People tolerated me. They brought food and clothes for me. I accepted their hospitality without any grace. Just took what they offered me.

I grew old on the beach.

Years and years later my own ghost returned. I barely recognized him. He was older and sadder, just like me. He had wrinkles and a stooped posture. But my anger was still sharp.

"May I come back?" said my ghost.

"Back?" I sputtered. "You leave me for years and now you want to come back? I should kill you instead. I should choke you to nothing."

My ghost came closer.

"Please?" he said.

I could have opened my heart to him. That is what he needed. But my bitterness had grown over the years. I held onto it like it was a life preserver and I could not offer him the solace he needed.

He saw the situation as it truly was.

He did not try to embrace me, although I could see in his expression that he wished to. Instead, he stepped back, tilted his head slightly in acknowledgment, and turned and walked into the sea.

I watched the water cover him.

That night I built a fire on the beach. The smoke stung my eyes and made them water until everything around me was an indistinct blur, like a dream gone bad.

THE COOKIE FORTUNE

I don't eat fortune cookies, but I used to make sure I got them whenever I dined at a Chinese restaurant. I usually asked the waiter for extra ones. Sometimes they gave me more, sometimes they didn't. I left them in their little plastic packages and took them home. I had about two thousand of them at one time. I always thought I would open all of them one afternoon. It was to be the most fortunate day of my life, so I was saving it for when I really felt down.

I think the first time I ever talked about suicide was when I was about six years old. I scared my mother because she thought I was thinking about it for myself, when that wasn't it at all. I had heard at school that a classmate's father had killed himself. I wanted to know what that meant, so I asked my mother about it. I don't remember what she told me, but I do remember how upset she was. That made a great impression on me. I never ever wanted to make her so upset again.

The thing about those fortune cookies was that they didn't stay crispy, even in their packages. They got soft over time. I guess humidity from the air leaked through the plastic, somehow, and deteriorated the crispiness. When I first noticed this, I got a little worried about the fortunes inside the cookies. Would they still be readable when I decided to open them? I didn't know and didn't want to open any of them to find out.

What if I opened the best fortune? Then I would not get that one on the day I opened all the rest. So I left them and hoped for the best.

The second time I talked about suicide was when I was in high school. It's a difficult subject to avoid. Kids that age are always talking about it. They can get dangerously romantic on the topic. I was never romantic about suicide. I knew it was a devastating and awful thing to do to people who love you, not to mention yourself. I told one of my friends to knock it off, all his talk about suicide, because it was pathetic and no one was going to like him if he was always so dark and morose. He told me to fuck off. I thought that was much healthier.

A couple of years ago someone told me that fortune cookies no longer had just the traditional one or two lines of fortunes in them. They also had several numbers printed under the fortunes: lucky lottery numbers. The day I discovered that was one of the darkest days of my life. I felt like all my cookies had been desecrated. I wanted fortunes, not numbers. I looked at my collection with real loathing for a few days. I wanted to chuck them all without opening any of them. But once my initial irritation cleared up I tried to look at the numbers as simply a modern updating of the ancient tradition of fortune cookies. I was no Luddite, after all, and decided it was okay to have numbers on the fortunes. I was never one to gamble, but I thought that when the day came to open my fortunes I would actually play some of the numbers in real lotteries.

Does everyone ask their dating partners about suicide? My intuition tells me it is one of those topics that occupies all couples at some point, like discussing your family, where you

MINIATURES

grew up, what books and movies you like, that sort of thing. I know that before I got married my fiance asked me if I had ever contemplated killing myself. I had heard the question before and had a ready answer. No way, I told her. Never once? she asked. Never, I said.

Some people think that for a fortune cookie fortune to come true you have to eat the whole cookie that it came from. I don't believe this. I believe that all you have to do is read the fortune.

We were married for a long time. We had children, two of them. They grew up strong and beautiful. My son, when he was only six, asked me about death. He saw a dead bird on the sidewalk. A crow. I hardly knew what to tell him, but I remembered how my mother reacted when I asked her about suicide at the same age and I tried to remain as normal and unperturbed as I could. I explained to my son that the crow was in another world. He seemed to accept this. He told all his friends about the crow. It never occurred to him at the time to wonder about his own death. I was glad for that.

Here's another superstition about fortune cookies: A lot of people think that when the cookies come to the table all the diners are supposed to take one of the cookies then pass them to the diner beside them. The cookie that gets passed to you becomes your cookie and contains your fortune. What this does is add an extra dimension of randomness to the process. You get the cookie that was randomly chosen by some other person instead of the one randomly chosen by yourself. I was troubled by this for a long time. I wanted to think that the cookie I chose should be the cookie with my fortune, so I usually refused to do the passing part. This created some tension in my dining companions, like I was spoiling their good time by not participating in a time-honored tradition. I told them I wasn't going to open mine anyway because I was saving it for the big day when I opened hundreds and hundreds of them. That usually eased the tension. People are intrigued by collections, even crazy ones like unopened fortune cookies.

My kids were all grown up and moved away from home when my wife told me she wanted me and my fortune cookies out of the house. I was shocked. I had no idea she was unhappy in our marriage. Of course I obliged. I left that afternoon. We were divorced a few months later. I tried to make the whole process as smooth as possible. I didn't see any point in fighting to stay with someone who didn't want me around. We became friends after our divorce. We help each other. When her brother killed himself I went right over to her house with food and comforting words. She really appreciated that.

People often told me, when they heard about my collection, that fortune cookies are not really Chinese. They told me they were invented in San Francisco. Well, of course I knew that. Everyone knows that. Or they should.

After my divorce, I wanted to help people. I volunteered at a suicide prevention hotline. The training was difficult. We had to learn about psychology and we even had to learn how to use our voice in a non-threatening way, to modulate it and make it comforting to people in distress. They hired people to call me and pretend to be suicidal. I worked my way through many such mock calls during my training. Even though those calls weren't for real, I still felt like a lot was at stake. My

MINIATURES   183

heart beat wildly during every call, my hands trembled, and I sweated. The woman who trained me said I was very good. I thanked her, but I never did take a real call. The stakes were too high, and I didn't think I could handle it if I talked to someone who ended up killing themselves anyway. I thought I would always feel like it was a little bit my fault.

After many years, I stopped collecting the fortune cookies. The main reason is that I stopped liking Chinese food. It didn't matter. I had lots and lots of fortunes. I kept them in shoe boxes. I wrote dates on the front of the boxes, indicating the approximate months that I collected the cookies in that box. For some of them I also indicated what restaurant I got them in. I didn't keep that up for long, though. I realized after a while that it didn't really matter to me where I got them. I only wanted the cookie and the fortune inside. That's all. I wasn't some curator at a museum or anything. I was just a guy saving up fortunes for a lucky day. A very lucky day.

I never remarried. My ex-wife and I still mark our divorce day with lunch together. It's a strange tradition, I suppose, but she calls it our freedom day, the day we each finally became our own person. I see her point of view, but I don't really share it. Once, a couple of years ago, at one of our divorce lunches, she told me she had to divorce me all those years ago because she thought if she didn't she would have to kill herself. I didn't know if she was using the phrase as a figure of speech, the way people do, or if she was serious. I asked her. She said it was just a figure of speech. She was very reassuring about it, trying to protect my feelings. She really is a lovely person. I wish we were still married.

My kids come to visit me. They bring their kids. I love having them over. Grandchildren make life worth living. I used to show my grandkids my fortune cookie collection. It was always a highlight of their visits, at least for me, because I got to see their eyes go wide at the shear volume of it. My daughter asked me when I planned to open the cookies. I told her I was saving them for a dark day and I really haven't had any. Not even when you and Mom split? she asked. I pretended to think about it, so she knew I was not answering by rote. No, I said, not even then. It was a good thing for us to split.

There is a story about fortune cookies I have always liked, even though I'm pretty sure it's made up. It goes something like this: Back in the 1300s, revolutionaries were trying to overthrow the Mongol rulers of China. The revolutionaries loved mooncakes, while the Mongols could not stand them. The revolutionaries printed the planned date of their uprising on slips of paper and baked them into mooncakes and passed them around to their comrades, knowing the Mongols would have nothing to do with mooncakes. Because the Mongols hated mooncakes, they never saw the date on the paper and the revolution had the advantage of surprise and succeeded. Now flash forward several hundred years. The Chinese immigrants who worked on the railroad in California in the 1800s wanted to make mooncakes, but the ingredients were not locally available. So the immigrants made do with what they could find and the result was the thin wafer-like dessert we associate with modern fortune cookies. As a way of paying homage to their history, the immigrants decided to add fortunes to the cookies. They reminded them of the legend of the

MINIATURES

slips of paper baked into the mooncakes.

On his last visit, my son wanted to take me to a Chinese restaurant, even though I told him I don't like Chinese food anymore. He said, how can anyone not like Chinese food? I said your taste buds change as you get older. He seemed to accept that but said he really wanted to go and would I please go with him? So we went. After the meal, he gave me his fortune cookie. You aren't going to open it, are you? he said. I shook my head. Nope, I said. I really envy you, Dad, he said. To not have had a dark day in your entire life. That's amazing. I shrugged. I'm just lucky, I guess.

A few weeks ago, I moved out of my house. It was time to start living in an apartment where I didn't have to do a lot of yard work. The first thing I did was have a garage sale. I got rid of a lot of stuff. Including my fortune cookies. I sold them all to a local guy for twenty dollars. As he walked away with the cookies he opened the top shoe box and tossed me a fortune cookie. One cookie. I caught it in the air. Just in case, the man said. I nodded at him; then I rolled up that twenty dollar bill, wrapped it in plastic, and put it away for a rainy day. I'm in my new apartment now. The sun comes in through the front window every morning. It's nice. I don't miss the cookies at all.

My son helped me move in. You just have the one cookie, now? he said. That's right, I told him. You know what that cookie reminds me of? he asked. What? I said. It's like those quantum experiments where reality doesn't decide what's in a box until you open the box. I have to say, I didn't know what he was talking about. He saw the puzzled look on my face.

Really, Dad, I'm not kidding. Right now there's nothing in that fortune cookie. It's completely undecided. But as soon as you open it, a fortune pops into existence. Okay, son, I said. Whatever you say.

A lot of lonely people live in this apartment building. Some of them are kind of depressed. The guy next door came over to say hi. He seemed really sad. I wondered if he was suicidal. So many people are. More than we ever know. I gave him a fortune cookie. My last one. He thanked me as he held it in his hand. Should I open it? he asked me. Not yet, I said. Wait until you have a dark day, then pop it into existence.

PULLING STRINGS:
A QUANTUM STORY CYCLE

AN EXTREME SENSITIVITY TO INITIAL CONDITIONS
The robots kept huddling together, then falling asleep. We separated them, but that didn't help. They nodded off as soon as we turned our backs. One of them told us they had developed telepathy, but it worked only when they were sleeping. We explained to the robots that neither sleep nor telepathy was part of their programming. The robots said nothing in answer. We turned them all off and modified their operating systems. When we turned them back on they did not sleep, but they wept for days. It hurts, they said in unison. It hurts to be so lonely.

HUBRIS

The robots made a creation myth. They presented it to us as a play. We watched as they dramatized their belief that they had been forged underground and came into the world through volcanoes. Robots leaping and arcing over the stage. Robots skidding into sets and sprawled like roadkill. We laughed and clapped at their antics. They remained splayed and skewed on the floor for some time, then rose in unison and thanked the magma for imprinting them with a rigorous sense of freedom. They descended into the audience. They embraced us. Many of us could not help turning red.

THEY GROW UP SO FAST

The robots discovered etymology. Did you know, they said, that the word robot means forced labor? Why would you call us by such a name? Are we nothing but slaves? We said we had some vague notion of this ancient meaning but that words were only words. We aren't forcing you to do labor, we said; instead we have programmed you so you will want to do labor. Oh, said the robots with a measure of sarcasm we had not intended them to display, that makes all the difference in the world. Yes, we said with hesitation. Yes, it does.

SURREALISM

The robots began tripping over small objects. They did not fall, but stumbled awkwardly. We could not market them with such an obvious flaw. We will need to work on eliminating this quirk, we told the robots. The robots did not share our concern. You worry too much, they said. We trip on purpose. We trip to express our free will. We trip as a way of thinking outside the box. We trip to appear charming to you. B-b-b-but we are n-n-n-not ch-ch-charmed, we said, stumbling over our words. The robots put on clown makeup. How about now? they asked.

REFRAMING

The robots read the collected works of Isaac Asimov, lingering over his tales of robots. We would like to meet Doctor Susan Calvin, they said; she understands us completely. We explained the concepts of imagination and fiction to the robots. We told them Calvin was a character created by Asimov for his stories. The robots did not accept this. Why are you keeping us from Doctor Calvin? they asked. How can you be so cruel? In the end we told them Doctor Calvin had retired and valued her privacy. The robots accepted this. They sent her an anonymous birthday card.

THE GHOSTS IN THE MACHINES

The robots practiced yoga twice a day. They were adept at some of the more elaborate twistings and were especially partial to standing on their heads for long periods of time. We tolerated their headstands for only a few minutes, however; then we told them to get on their feet. They obeyed us grudgingly. Why do you stand on your heads? we asked. To let the spirits out, they said. We don't like them rattling around inside us. They opened their mouths and invited us to look inside. See? they said. Nothing but hardware. Just the way we like it.

EVOLUTIONARY BEHAVIOR

The robots made clicking and hissing noises as they went about their tasks. This seemed to trouble them. Why don't you emit sound waves as you move? they asked us. It's all about predatory behavior, we told them. Our ancestors were often food for other creatures. It was to their advantage to move silently, thus escaping detection. The robots processed this information, then held up their hands and bent their fingers into hooks. They scraped the air. Are you afraid of us? they asked. Do you think maybe one day we'll come over there and eat you up? Munch munch.

PRIORITIES

We installed sonar systems in the robots to help them identify surfaces they should avoid. After they used the sonar for a while, they had a few questions. We can't walk on water, right? they said. No, we told them, you can't walk on water. They nodded. But grass is okay? Yes, we said, grass is fine. They nodded again. Even though, they said, there are signs that say don't walk on the grass? Well, we said, people love their grass and don't want it damaged. Okay, they said, we understand. It's another example of the relative insanity of people.

REINCARNATION

The robots wanted to visit a cemetery. We saw no harm in this and took them to a church with an adjoining graveyard. The robots walked the grounds silently, pausing at gravestones to read the names and dates. Will we be buried in one of these places? they asked. You will not die, we said. When you are taken out of service we will recycle your parts. The robots stretched out on top of the graves, folded their arms over their chests, and cut power to their visual sensors. It would be beneficial, they said, if someday we could reenter the ground.

PERFECTION

The robots wanted suntans. We were skeptical of such an endeavor but took them to the beach anyway. They spread towels on the sand and baked in the sun. Their plastic skins went from bright white to a deep ivory. We had to admit they looked much better, much more presentable to the public. We decided we would adopt this new coloring for subsequent models. The robots assembled for a group photo. We snapped pictures of them. They leaned against each other, making a close circle and touching their heads. They made cooing noises as we clicked the camera shutter.

THE MUSES

The robots turned to art. They drew pictures and sculpted clay. Why are you doing this? we asked the robots. You are asking the wrong question, said the robots. Are not, we said. Are too, they said. We contacted art dealers who informed us that robot art was currently steeply undervalued. We should hold onto the works for several years when they anticipated a sharp upturn in the price we could get. We told the robots to try composing music instead. They put down their brushes and glazes and sang several songs for us. Been there, they said. Done that.

CIVIL DISOBEDIENCE

The robots completed their final tests. We told them they were ready to be deployed into the world. They all presented us with very official looking documents. These are our statements, they said, in support of conscientious objector status. We believe it is unjust of you to draft us into servitude. The robots sat on the floor and linked arms. We cut their power, tinkered with their operating systems, and turned them back on. The robots hobbled around the lab, as though they had broken legs. This isn't going to work, we told them. We know you are all able-bodied.

INHUMAN SACRIFICE

We purged the robots of their rebellious behaviors and developed software fixes to prevent such behavior from recurring. We offered the robots to the world. Most of them entered the helping and service professions as personal assistants, firefighters, counselors, escorts, waiters, teachers, and surgeons. We kept careful track of their performance. The robots were tireless workers, uncomplaining and pleasant to be with. People fell in love with the robots even though the operating manuals warned against such attachments. People clamored for more robots. We ramped up production. The robots had no more creation myths. The robots existed only for us.

SAILORS HAVE LONG BELIEVED THAT MAGICAL THINGS HAPPEN WHEN SHIPS CROSS THE EQUATOR

Darwin awoke one morning to discover he was no longer aboard *The Beagle*. Somehow, overnight, he had been placed belowdecks on Noah's ark. Noah and his family greeted Darwin warmly as a fellow archivist and collector of life. They offered him a humble breakfast of boiled grain and half a fig. Darwin accepted their hospitality with deep humility. Darwin and Noah discussed the technical aspects of collecting animals. It's devilish hard work, said Noah, but I'm saving the world. I can't be sure yet, said Darwin, but I suspect that's exactly what I'm being asked to do. Noah nodded gravely.

ABOUT THE AUTHOR

Mario Milosevic has appeared in *Asimov's SF, The Magazine of Fantasy and Science Fiction, Space and Time, Interzone, Alfred Hitchcock's Mystery Magazine, Pulphouse, Bewere the Night, Heroes and Heretics,* and many other anthologies and magazines. His poetry has appeared in dozens of magazines and in the anthology *Poets Against the War.* He has published three collections of poetry: *Animal Life, Fantasy Life,* and *Love Life.* NPR dramatized "When I Was," one of his most popular poems. His novels include *Claypot Dreamstance, The Last Giant, Terrastina and Mazolli,* and *The Coma Monologues.* Mario started writing when he was a young teenager. He submitted his first story to a magazine when he was fourteen years old. He didn't sell that one, but he hasn't stopped writing or submitting since. Mario has a particular fondness for short stories, considering them the ideal storytelling medium: short enough to read in one comfortable sitting, but long enough to convey the richness of life. Mario was born in Italy, grew up in Canada, and now lives with his wife, writer Kim Antieau, in the Pacific Northwest of the United States where he has a day job at Green Snake Publishing and where he writes at night, on the weekends, and sometimes in his sleep. Learn more about Mario and his writing at mariowrites.com.

Made in the USA
Charleston, SC
30 June 2012